THE

HUNGUR

CHRONICLES

Samhain

Edited by:
TERRIE LEIGH RELF
&
ROBERT BELLAM

1

THE STAFF OF THE HUNGUR CHRONICLES

EDITOR: Terrie Leigh Relf
ASSOCIATE EDITOR: Robert Bellam
WEBMASTER: H David Blalock

Cover art "Screaming Lady" by Nick Sea & Suzie Sea
Cover design by Marcia Borell

Vol. II, No.2   November 2023
The Hungur Chronicles is published semiannually on the 1st day of May and November in the United States of America by Hiraeth Publishing, P.O. Box 1248, Tularosa, NM, 88352. Copyright 2023 by Hiraeth Publishing. All rights revert to authors and artists upon publication except as noted in selected individual contracts. Nothing may be reproduced in whole or in part without written permission from the authors and artists. Any similarity between places and persons mentioned in the fiction or semi-fiction and real places or persons living or dead is coincidental. Writers and artists guidelines are available online at www.hiraethsffh.com. Guidelines are also available upon request from Hiraeth Publishing, P.O. Box 1248, Tularosa, NM, 88352, if request is accompanied by a self-addressed #10 envelope with a first-class US stamp. Editor: Tyree Campbell.

Support the First Amendment and the Small Independent Publishers! Remember, our right to publish is your right to read.

Contents

Features

Stories

A Note from Your Editors, Terrie Leigh Relf and Robert Bellam

Welcome to the fourth issue of *Hungur Chronicles!* We certainly hope you enjoy reading this issue as much as we did curating it. Here's to vampires of all ilks, the stranger the better. We have some wonderfully quirky and literary tales for you—including extra-terrestrial jaunts.

(And yes, the King's English is welcomed here.)

—Terrie Leigh Relf, Lead Editor

The fourth edition of *Hungur Chronicles* is a fascinating journey through the imagination of a group of gifted writers. This compilation explores the world of Vampires. These are not just your usual Neck Drainers; the ingenuity of those who submitted has created Vampires with unique needs. They nourish themselves—not only to maintain life, but to increase their energetic and sexual needs . . . And yes, as well as their need to connect with others. In other words, these are NOT your usual Vampires. Put your imagination to work and submit your Vampire story—with a twist—today. In the meantime, please enjoy our latest issue!

—Robert Bellam Co-Editor

Symbiosis
Tyree Campbell

On Earth the butterfly might have been given another name, but here on Malache, Frange named it the *Pseudolepido purpurea*, for its spectacular wings. She had found it investigating a red globe-shaped flower with thick petals wrapped like cabbage. Laying a finger in front of it, she allowed it to climb aboard; she then lifted it closer to her face for examination. It stabbed her with two fangs that protruded from the mandibles, and returned to the flower, where another stab where the stem joined the globe caused floral nectar to leak out.

> globe flower dies
> name changes
> *Pseudolepido vampirensis*

The Cleaner
Marcia A. Borell

Blood. The smell of it excites me. The scent of iron is delicate. Perhaps a final sacrifice from an anemic anorexic girl. The heaps of size two dresses scattered across the floor tell her tale.

From the looks of things, she slit her wrists and then played patty cake with the wall. The forensic team packed up and left. The rest of the job is up to me. I get down on my hands and knees, thrust out my salivating tongue, and lick the bloody hand prints from the wall.

> mirror reveals me
> smacking my bloody lips
> my victimless crime

Sabit the Sumerian

a novella by Tyree Campbell
inspired by the Epic of Gilgamesh!

Cursed and banished to the dung-filled streets of
Uruk by the king for whom she was once a

companion, Sabit must now sell herself in order to survive. Near starving, and bearing the mark of the *lillu*, or vampire, she is plagued by dreams of the ancient ones who dwell beyond the mountains of Elam.

Sabit meets a girl around her own age, a kind girl with brilliant blue eyes, who asks what no other woman has ever asked: "What are you selling?" That night, Sabit's new friend comes to her in a dream, asking for that which cannot be taken, but freely given. The girl is Shala, Daughter of Ereshkigal, Goddess of the Underworld. Vampire.

Thousands of years pass. One night, Sabit, now known as Adrienne Bouchard, meets a man in a park, and her life is irrevocably changed once more. His name is Ian Cullen, a recently widowed archaeologist, with a young daughter auspiciously named Shala.

When the Daughter of Ereshkigal returns, she commands Adrienne to make a choice: Kill or turn Ian and his daughter. How will she choose? Will Adrienne sacrifice herself for two humans? Are they nothing but cattle after all?

https://www.hiraethsffh.com/product-page/sabit-the-sumerian-by-tyree-campbell

I Wear Shades Everywhere I Go Is Not Because I Think I'm That Cool

Francis W. Alexander

Rumor was that a substance arrived in a meteor, like a Body Snatcher's movie. The joke going around featured aliens wanting to speed up our intellectual development.

I remember when I transitioned. Her name was Flo, a scorching hot babe. Wearing Taboo perfume, she stopped by my apartment late one night.

As we lay on the couch, Flo stared into my hazel eyes. She nearly drained me of all my knowledge.

My fortune came two weeks ago at Big Jim's bar. Drunk, my victim took off her shades. Her knowledge was scrumptious.

> vigilance
> wearing my green sunglasses
> wherever I go

Beware of the Streets

Andrage Benedick

Dusk fell above Howard's three-story apartment building. The people inside were winding down after a long day, fetching their dinners and sitting down in front of the TV.

The building, with its brown brick, resembled a dropping from one of the big skyscrapers in the distance. Howard detested it since he moved, with the ever-growing pile of garbage blocking the side door and the noisy punker from the ground floor.

But at least it was safe. Warm. With running water and his family of cacti, that he so lovingly collected over the years, bathing in the sunlight on his shelf.

At least, it used to be that way. Until Howard got fired. Getting fired meant he couldn't pay his rent, which got him kicked out of his apartment, forcing him to spend the night in the twenty-four hour diner two blocks down.

Yes, he did get drunk, and yes, he did cry. Not so much for himself, you see, but for his plants. His fairy castle cactus was dying in a dumpster somewhere, tossed out by his former landlord.

He tried to take them with him, but he had nowhere to go. Family? None. Friends? None. All he had were his cacti, and a tent that he bought with what little money he had left. The plan was to camp out for a few days until he can get back on his feet, and the plan worked.

Until the cops confiscated the tent after a few hours of camping in the bushes of Central Park. For loitering of all things! Like he was there because he had nothing better to do. Well, he didn't have anything better to do, but still.

Thus tent-less, cacti-less, jobless, and a half dozen other signifiers for a lack of possessions, he found himself at the place he called home just a day ago: his old, smelly, rundown building.

Across the street, he saw another man, curled in the fetus position, and using old pizza boxes as a blanket. Howard gave him a nod. The man nodded back.

With the nightly chill approaching, he realised this will be his first night of sleeping on the sidewalk. Cozying up next to the dumpster, and covering himself with some wet newspaper, he drifted off to that place between dreams and hard concrete.

Howard woke up. Someone was moaning. He lifted his head, his whole body aching from sleeping on the concrete.

Someone screamed. He tried to blink away his fatigue, but sleep was still heavy in his eyes. Focusing, he looked through the alleyway. The lamp lights made small, circular dents into the darkness, like looking into a hole-ridden sock.

Howard heard raspy breaths rattling like a chain. His heart was pounding, his stomach twisting itself into a knot. A smell of iron wafted up into his nose, and that is when he saw it.

A lifeless, crimson-covered body was being dragged by a tall figure. It weaved in-and-out of the darkness through the lights, revealing its long, misshapen limbs.

It moved with unnatural smoothness, as its joints twisted and turned. Looking at it made him sick. More than the screams, more than seeing the battered body of a man. He did everything he could to stop himself from gagging.

The creature stopped, and with it, Howard's breath. Did it see him? Is he next? Is this how he will spend his last moments? With his face down in the muck, covered by wads of newspaper?

A part of him urged himself to run. He would have if he had any feeling left inside his legs. Instead, the fear paralyzed him, rendering him immobile.

The creature turned. Howard could feel it looking for him, all the way from across the street, with its beady, yellow eyes.

Did it find him? Is this it?

His heart was jumping out of his chest, his vision focusing only on those eyes, those hungry, hungry eyes . . .

It lifted its head up, sniffed the air, looking in his general direction. It just stood there, waiting. Waiting. Waiting.

It turned, dragging the other man's lifeless body with it.

The next morning, he got kicked awake by one of his previous neighbours. At her mention of calling the police, Howard mumbled a halfhearted apology, and walked off. The concrete wasn't kind to his body, leaving him feeling groggy and broken.

A quick wash in the public fountain later, he stared at his reflection in the water. An image of the creature seared into his mind's eye. "What a nightmare," he said, brushing away his hair, playing it through and through in his head.

Howard decided that his night full of terrors – no doubt produced by a hangover, and a bed of concrete – were no reason to hold him off from getting on his feet.

Spending the day to search for jobs, he took every "Help Wanted" sign as an opportunity to better himself. Though most gave him a polite refusal, he did find a position in an established chain restaurant. The manager took pity on him, on account of having a kind heart and a relatable experience. It was only flipping burgers, but it was better than nothing.

That still left him with a particular issue of housing. Through sheer luck, he found an ad for a homeless shelter a few blocks down the road. The ad was in a discarded magazine, intended for volunteers, but hey, a bed is a bed.

At least there he won't have to worry about having another one of those nightmares.

The shelter, once a high school gymnasium, was filling up to capacity faster than Howard expected. He managed to secure himself a spot at the northern wall, next to a scruffy, older guy, who seemed lucid enough to not pose a threat.

A volunteer, a middle-aged woman with red hair, came over to give them each a blanket. She played with a curl of her deep red hair as she spoke to Howard, her genuine smile feeling like chicken soup for the soul.

He told her about his cacti family, how she reminded him of the Easter cactus. It is a lesser known species, which blooms in early spring with beautiful crimson flowers, matching the colour of her hair. He even told her his favourite cacti joke – "What did one cactus say to the other? You prickle my fancy!" – to which she laughed, making Howard feel a spark between them.

Once the volunteer was gone, the old man correctly ascertained that Howard was new on the streets. "No one with that much good spirits has been living in the muck for long," he said, which Howard took as a compliment, and a sign of better things to come.

George, the old man, turned out to be an upstanding guy, tossed on the street by a family tragedy. He imparted on Howard some street wisdom, like how to get money and where to spend it. Surprisingly, the best use for the money was a gym membership. It would offer all the hot showers he needed, and allowed him to keep busy while looking to get back up on his feet.

It was the boredom, George said, alongside fatigue and hopelessness, that drew many of the street denizens to drugs. Howard made a mental note of that, though he was only half listening, instead thinking about buying an Easter cactus as a present for the volunteer.

But it was his next piece of advice that twisted a knot in Howard's stomach.

"Be careful on the streets, boy. There is a menace out there, and it's worse than some preppy psychos trying to pay you for all kinds of twisted shit."

"And that is?" Howard asked.

George leaned closer. "Vampires."

Howard's first instinct was to laugh. I mean, Vampires? Really?

His reaction, however, was overridden by an image of a tall figure, its beady, yellow eyes, staring at him. Waiting.

He felt sick, his face cringing as he started to relive the night.

"Holy shit, you've seen one?" George asked, his voice full of surprise. "And you're alive? How?"

Howard took a moment to collect his thoughts, to push away the image of those eyes away from him. "I was sleeping by a dumpster. There was another guy across the street. He . . . he didn't make it."

George nodded, brushing his beard. "If it gets on your trail, you're done for. They're bigger, stronger, faster. You must have masked your scent well enough."

Howard shook his head. "I thought vampires were a stupid story about counts and maidens living in castles and sleeping in coffins?"

George shrugged. "Well they ain't. They hunt the homeless. I've seen them a couple of times myself. Always from afar and while they were already feeding, though. Those eyes . . ." he said, shivering.

"And why isn't anyone doing anything, then?"

"Like who? The police? The government? They don't care about us, man. They're probably happy they have someone to take out the trash from the street, so to speak."

Howard started shaking. Those . . . things. They're real? How? Where did they come from?

George slapped him on the shoulder. "Relax, man. They don't attack big groups. The shelter is the safest place you can be, ain't no vampire stupid enough to come here. They'd be exposed in a second."

That made Howard feel better, though not much. He turned away from George, curling up in his bed,

13

pulling the blanket over his head. He had to endure this for a few more days, and then he'll be able to get a place of his own and not worry about . . . *vampires*.

In his dreams, Howard was running. Block after block he ran, always looking back, seeing the shadow of the creature on the walls. He heard that chain-rattling breath, the smell of iron overwhelming him, footsteps on his heel.

He startled himself awake with heavy breaths. George was making a gargling sound, and Howard turned to tell him to knock it off.

His eyes were wide open and unfocused, as if paralysed, blood spurting out of his mouth like a fountain in the park. On him, biting down on his neck, was a silhouette of a person, its arms long and sinewy.

The person stopped. Howard froze. It turned, facing him. Its face twisted and stretched. Blood covering its elongated maw, its mouth, brandishing a set of razor sharp fangs.

Howard recognised its red hair. *The volunteer,* he thought, as two beady, yellow eyes stared at him.

It smiled. Then jumped.

Howard rolled off the bed, landing on its side. Scrambling to his feet, he ran as fast as he could, his legs feeling a sense of déjà vu. He jumped over the beds, over the sleeping people, his breath hoarse and wild, as he ran for the fire exit to the side.

He didn't dare to look back, but he could hear footsteps. Delicate like silk on the hardwood floor, a whooshing sound as it traversed the terrain with ease.

Nobody is waking up. Why isn't anyone waking up?!

He reached the door. He slammed into it, throwing it open, then slamming it shut. He took a two-by-four at the side, jamming it into the door.

Taking a step back, he watched the door with heavy breaths, his heart beating almost out of his chest. Something rammed into them from the other side,

14

indenting the doors and bending the rod. But the doors stayed closed.

Slam. Slam. Slam. The rod held somehow, but for how long? Howard didn't intend to find out. He turned, dashing into the alleyways, hoping for a saviour to spare his life.

The darkness was heavy, but his eyes adjusted. He could barely see the edges of buildings and gutters filled with garbage juice. Remembering George's words about throwing them off his scent, he searched for a dumpster.

He felt like he was back in the dream. Running for his life, seeing the creature's shadow everywhere he looked. A sadness welled up in him, realizing that if he doesn't find a place to hide, he is done for.

There!

Finally, he found a dumpster. He jumped in, tearing apart bags of garbage, and stuffing discarded food in his sleeves, pockets, and pants. The smell would make him sick if the adrenaline in his veins wasn't pushing him on.

He lifted the lid ever so slightly, enough that he could peek outside.

The floor was wet, liquid oozing into his shoes. His arms were already beginning to feel heavy, and an eerie quiet settled into the alley.

A tall figure with arms stretching to the ground walked past his alleyway. It was walking with a hunch and on all fours, swinging like a branch in the wind. It had its nose high up into the air, sniffing.

It looked into his alley. Howard's pulse stopped.

The red stain on its face, the last remnant of George's life, was still there. Looking at it, Howard felt like he was going to pass out, his body shaking from the fear, the cold, the disgust.

The creature moved, continuing past his alleyway and leaving his sight.

Howard wished he would feel relieved, but he didn't. Instead, he felt a panic. The kind that gripped your heart and squeezed at every sound, at every light, at every movement, and every thought that strayed too far.

His eyes stuck to the alleyway, refusing to look away. What was that? Was it the creature? The same one? A different one?

Nothing happened. Was it a rat? Or only his imagination?

He felt the weariness settle in his bones. The fatigue bit into his brain, hooking it by the cerebellum. It hung there, laughing at him as he waited inside of a dumpster, too afraid to move even a muscle.

It felt like he hadn't shut his eyes in hours. They were burning from the dryness, making Howard feel the grooves of the tiny blood vessels in his eyes. He wanted to close them so, so badly. But then they would get him. Slaughter him on the streets like some common rat.

He couldn't let that happen. He wouldn't. He was too young, with so much to live for. He wanted to experience a new career, maybe get himself a girlfriend. And more cacti. Definitely more cacti.

So many possibilities. So many things still left unsaid and undone.

He watched from underneath the lid of the dumpster, his thoughts haunting him through the night. Watching for the creature's return. Twisting and turning himself within the confines of his mind, as he spiraled into the depths of fear and regret.

Sunlight creeped up on the alley, making the puddles of garbage juice shimmer. In the crisp cold of morning, the warm fumes from a nearby manhole started rising.

It took him a few minutes to realize that it was morning. He had survived the night.

Howard almost screamed with joy. He made it. He is alive!

He ran out the dumpster, rushing through the alleys. "I'm alive," he screamed from the top of his lungs, arms reaching high into the sky.

He rushed into a busy street. "I am alive," he shouted to the half-asleep commuters on their way to work. He ran up to a businessman dressed in a sharp blue suit. "They didn't get me," he said, hugging the man, who pushed him away in disgust.

"They didn't get me, but they might tonight," he said to a young woman, following her down the street. She was shielding herself from him, putting her bag between her face and his, but he did not care. "I need a place for tonight . . . Could I sleep at your place? Please? Just for tonight?"

He pestered the pedestrians, pleading with them to let him sleep in their home. None of them wanted anything to do with him.

He knelt on the pavement, letting the sun warm his cold body. He closed his eyes, feeling the pleasant burn beneath his eyelids. His arms felt heavy and his feet were wet from standing in the dumpster.

He smiled, feeling the sunshine on his face. Lulled by the light, the warmth, he found himself drifting away into sleep.

Something lifted him up by the arms. With the last of his strength, he opened his eyes.

An angel was carrying him. An angel in a police uniform.

Howard awoke in a holding cell. He saw through a small window that dusk had fallen. He was lying on an uncomfortable wooden bench, though it was miles ahead of not sleeping in a dumpster.

He readjusted, looking around. It was a small holding cell, and he was the only one occupying it. White bars and beige brick surrounded him, and for the first time in a while, he felt safe.

Though to be honest, he also felt stupid. He could have gotten himself arrested at the end of a day, and he would get to spend the night in a cushy cell, far away from those creatures.

His pulse quickened. Even a single thought about them was enough to send a panic running through his system again, making his intestines wriggle.

They were eating the homeless and nobody seemed to care. But the police should care, shouldn't they?

Howard shuddered.

The doors to his cell slid open and two tall officers walked in. "Look who's finally awake," one of them said.

"I am. Thank you for bringing me here," Howard said, jumping on his feet. "Listen, I would like to report something, something dangerous. It's out there on the streets, killing-"

"Something is killing people, eh?" the other one said, prompting the both of them to laugh.

"You don't understand," Howard said, taking a step toward them. The officer kicked him, sending him flying back onto the bench.

"Oh, I understand completely," an officer said, leaning in closer to him. He smiled, his hands stretching down to the floor. His lips parted, pushing out a maw of sharp fangs, stretching out his face.

His eyes flashed, turning yellow. "But you need to understand that it's dinner time!"

The Derelict
Gary Davis

NASA *Spaceship Hawking* fired its thrusters and eased into a high orbit around the blue, gas-giant planet Neptune. Its orbit now closely paralleled the path of a spherical body thought for decades to be a small Neptunian moon. Captain Russell of *Hawking*, however, could clearly see that this silvery, perfectly round sphere was artificial, not natural. He quickly barked orders to Kim and Carlos to suit up and get ready to investigate. In the meantime, he brought the *Hawking* to within less than a thousand yards of the target body.

Kim and Carlos were both First Lieutenants in the U. S. Space Force, and this was their first voyage to the outer Solar System. They had previously worked in exploration, terraforming and mining at NASA bases on Mars. This was also the first long-distance venture for *Spaceship Hawking*, named after the famed British theoretical physicist and cosmologist, Stephen Hawking, who had lived a century-and-a-half earlier. Stephen Hawking, despite suffering for decades from a paralyzing, ALS-type motor neurone disease, was widely known for his theories about black holes, books on astronomy aimed at a popular audience, and warnings about the danger of Earthly contact with aliens.

Kim and Carlos soon finished their spacesuit preparations and exited the main airlock of *Spaceship Hawking*. They used their powerful jetpacks to steer a path towards the strange shiny sphere. At least their communications were working fine, and they were breathing easily.

Kim spoke up. "What do you suppose this big thing up ahead is? I am surprised Captain Russell didn't give us any briefing on it ahead of time."

Carlos replied, anxiously. "That's a good question, Kim. This investigation does seem a bit rushed. One of my shipmates back on *Hawking* suggested that the sphere might be a spaceport secretly built and launched by China or Russia, with the objective of controlling the outer Solar System."

"Maybe a Death Star," said Kim. The two chuckled.

As Kim and Carlos approached the spherical body, it became increasingly apparent to them that this object was no spaceport from Earth. First, the size was truly massive, over a thousand yards in diameter. No spaceport originating from Earth was remotely this large. No wonder it had been mistaken for a moon by earlier probes passing near Neptune. The shininess of the sphere magnified its size because of reflected sunlight, although the Sun appeared very dim from the distance of Neptune.

Something else looked strange as the two NASA-nauts closed in. The huge sphere was dented with thousands of pockmarks from small meteoroid collisions. There were also some moderately large and jagged holes in the metallic surface. Perhaps the object had been hit by numerous rocks and dust bits from the several faint "rings" around Neptune. In any case, the evidence of extensive natural impact damage implied that the target body had been in the Solar System for a very long time and since before the Space Age on Earth. Kim wondered if it had been lurking here for centuries or even thousands of years. She blurted out, "Look at all those holes! Anybody or anything living here has been long dead or long gone. This is a derelict."

"Yes", responded Carlos. "This beat-up thing is really ancient and a big mystery, too."

The two lieutenants received an order from Captain Russell. Sounding impatient and imperious, he urged them to find an airlock or other entrance into the target sphere and commence exploring the interior, being careful not to come into direct contact with any biological material or suspected organisms. Carlos and Kim replied in the affirmative.

First, Kim and Carlos jetted off horizontally in opposite directions around the huge circumference of this sphere that was now obviously alien to the Solar System. They met on the opposite side without finding an airlock entrance. The two then moved up and down the surface in a zig-zag fashion toward successively higher altitudes in opposite directions. Finally, Carlos located what seemed to be a concave airlock about midway between the sphere's "equator" and its upper pole. He and Kim applied their blasting-torch tool to the perimeter of the airlock but were unable to make any headway penetrating the unknown metallic material it was made of. They only generated a shower of sparks. It appeared to be harder than diamond and wasn't like any substance they had encountered on either Earth or Mars.

Carlos and Kim shook their heads and rested for a minute. Carlos suggested, "Hey, let's find a really large meteorite hole somewhere on this body and see if we can get inside that way. Some big rocks did penetrate whatever the main surface is made of."

"Ok", said Kim. "However, those holes will no doubt have sharp, jagged edges. We have to be very careful going in and out. We don't want to rip our spacesuits."

The two climbed upward towards the pole of the sphere but did not see any large meteorite holes. They carefully stepped around the small holes and fissures they encountered. Carlos and Kim continued downwards on the opposite side. After a few minutes, they found themselves staring into a massive oval cavity about five yards across. They reported this discovery to Captain Russell and then proceeded to enter the derelict, being careful not to brush up against the edges of the hole.

Kim and Carlos were immediately amazed by what they saw inside the massive alien sphere. It was almost like a misshapen honeycomb. There were tunnels branching off in all directions. They looked very curved in structure and not flat and level as in a typical spaceport from Earth. Taking a closer look inside one sort of "hallway," the two NASA-nauts could see that it was a dull blackish- gray in color and appeared to follow a winding, up and down, or sinuous path. In addition, this particular tunnel was both extremely tall and very wide compared to passages on Earthborn ships, far taller than a typical eight-to-ten-foot height that humans were accustomed to.

Kim remarked, "This passageway doesn't look like it was made for walking through as humans would normally do. I am wondering if, whatever creatures resided here, maybe they flew through this tunnel. Perhaps the up and down curves were intended to keep those beings from flying too fast within the confines of the spaceport."

"Good point," replied Carlos. "Einstein said that space is curved. We Earthlings are habituated to an environment of linearity that may be totally at odds to what certain alien species adapt to."

Kim and Carlos paused for a minute. They turned around and exited the rather tiring and disorienting passageway they were in. They then selected a more centrally located tunnel to investigate. This passage, however, was structured in a similar fashion to the first tunnel they had visited. It fortunately didn't curve up and down much, but wound around side-to-side a lot. The dark walls were not flat but wavy—covered in rippled undulations that resembled the surface of a lake. The two astronauts plowed ahead this time. Carlos complained, "I would get such a splitting headache if I had to walk around in a weird curvy place like this all the time."

"Likewise," said Kim. The two began to slow down their breathing so as to conserve the oxygen in their tanks.

After fifteen minutes inside this second winding tunnel, Kim and Carlos spied large chambers on the left and right sides. They shined their powerful lithium-ion LED flashlights from side-to-side and up and down. The left-hand room contained several colossal, spaced-out niches, each one octagonal in outline, sharply concave in depth, and light gray in color. Along the wall of the right-hand room were lined up huge vats, perhaps twenty feet tall, made of some kind of transparent material. They appeared to contain varying amounts of a black liquid.

Kim stated, "Maybe this is some type of rocket fuel or possibly something organic. Let's have a closer look."

"If this is organic or biological matter, we have to be very cautious and follow a special protocol," Carlos reminded Kim. "But yes, we need to do a close-up inspection."

Carlos and Kim slowly walked up to one of the vats in the middle of the row. They lightly tapped on the surface of the container. Although transparent, it did not appear to be glass. It was either a very hard and dense plastic or perhaps some unknown metallic substance. The two astronauts tapped harder and noticed a slight vibration of the material within. It therefore seemed to be a thick, viscous liquid. Carlos remarked, "You know, Kim, this heavy black liquid might have been a different color a long time ago, given the apparent age of the derelict ship. Let's see if we can find out something about its composition, the elements and compounds in it. Maybe there's something organic here, like you suggested—organic but now decayed."

Kim looked up and down the vat. Near the bottom, about a foot-and-a-half above the floor, she noticed a narrow, dark tube sticking out very slightly from the vat wall, less than half-an-inch. She and Carlos bent down to look at it. They could see an opening at their end of the tube. Perhaps there was a residue of the vat liquid at the rim of the mouth. Kim had training in biochemistry;

Carlos had a little bit. Kim pulled out a small chemistry scanner from a spacesuit pocket and held it several inches from the tube opening. Neither one of them touched the tube mouth itself.

After half-a-minute, Kim pulled her scanner away and looked down at the screen. Her eyebrows arched upward.

"Wow, what did you get?" asked Carlos. Anything organic?" "Well," replied Kim, "most of the readings here are not comprehensible, stuff I don't recognize. There seems to be a bunch of carbon, nitrogen, oxygen, and hydrogen compounds that have likely decomposed over a long period of time, which makes sense. However, the scanner is also showing evidence of the protein heme, which is part of hemoglobin and binds with oxygen. We know all about hemoglobin on Earth, of course."

"Yes, we know all about that," said Carlos, seemingly distracted. "Very interesting."

Carlos suddenly held up his hand and looked down at his oxygen tank meter. "Oops, we need to get back to the *Hawking* soon. My oxygen tank is starting to run low."

"Yes, mine too," said Kim.

Carlos contacted Captain Russell and informed him of their oxygen supply situation and that they would be returning shortly. He said to Russell, "Kim picked up, according to our safety standards, some chemistry scanner evidence of decomposed and residual organics here. We'll give you a full report when we return."

Kim and Carlos, moving more quickly now, returned to the entrance of the large tunnel. When they arrived there, Kim said, panting, "Hey, wait a second. I'm not sure we should exit just yet. I think we should do a brief reconnaissance of a few other tunnel entrances to see if there is anything else significant to report on. It would look better for the Captain's log and NASA report. We haven't even found the command-and-control center or the engine room. We should have enough oxygen for a short detour before going back to the Hawking."

"Ok Kim," said Carlos, hesitantly and shaking his head a bit. I suppose I'm game for that. Let's get going and keep our breathing under control."

The two began checking out other passageway openings within the enigmatic derelict ship. They obviously wouldn't have time to canvas all of them. After a few minutes, they noticed what appeared to be a faint, blinking red light coming from the end of one tunnel several hundred feet away from the large one they had already investigated. This tunnel was much smaller in height and width, not much taller than the two astronauts. It was also level and straight, not winding sideways or undulating up and down. The passage apparently took just one shallow bend, not far ahead of them, in the direction of the flashing red light. Carlos exclaimed, "This tunnel almost seems to be made for humans. Let's investigate that light right now."

Carlos and Kim quickly traversed the short passageway. They halted directly in front of a broad, high-ceilinged room with an open door. They could see the red light suspended below the ceiling, apparently in the middle of the large chamber. The strangest thing Carlos and Kim noticed, judging by diffuse lighting effects, was that the room appeared to contain an atmosphere; it was progressively denser towards the center. However, this atmosphere did not seem to extend out into the hallway in front of the door. Some kind of central or peripheral force was holding it within the room.

The two explorers cautiously entered the room. Kim pulled out an ADM—Atmosphere Detection Meter—and held it up in front of her suit helmet. After she got a quick reading, she said to Carlos, "This air does contain oxygen, but less than what we are used to on Earth. Plus, there are some other compounds here that I don't recognize, and they might be toxic. Let's stay safe and remain helmeted."

"Yes, great idea," said Carlos.

The first thing that Kim and Carlos noticed inside was an array of monumental, glossy black statues in varying poses along either side of the door. "Amazing!" exclaimed Carlos. "These things remind me of that ancient Cretaceous flying reptile, the Pteranodon, a relative of dinosaurs. Some of them had huge wing spans of over twenty feet. These statue heads do look different, toothy and a lot less protruding, and there are claws in addition to wings. I see a resemblance in the body, however."

Kim remarked, "It seems like the aliens who lived here had a history of biological evolution at least partly parallel to ours, maybe their own dinosaur era. I remember back on Earth that kids all like dinosaurs. Of course, a few dinosaurs survived the Cretaceous extinction event and eventually downsized to become birds, and birds can be very intelligent. This place is almost like an exhibit hall or museum."

The two inched towards the center of the room. The atmosphere was very heavy and foggy here. They could make out, just barely, the outlines of a long and wide, octagonal-shaped container. "Here is another exhibit," said Kim. They peered down at the top, and Kim tapped lightly on the surface. "This material feels like glass and maybe not real thick," she said.

Carlos responded, "Okay, but it's more translucent than transparent. I can't make out any detailed shapes inside."

Suddenly, the glass shattered, serrated claws ripped, and pincer fangs sucked. In one minute, the two Earthlings were a collapsed shell of bone and skin.

Two tall vampires stood up, their heads almost grazing the ceiling, and slowly unfurled ten-foot wings.

They exchanged satiated smiles. This was their first fresh blood in five thousand years.

Blood Sampler
By David Lee Summers &
Lee Clark Zumpe

Two of the finest minds in the genres have amalgamated their resources and imaginations to come up with some of the gothiest and goofiest vampire flash fiction this side of Bucharest. David Lee Summers, of *Tales of the Talisman* and *Heirs of the New Earth* fame, and Lee Clark Zumpe, mild-mannered reporter for a daily metro-Floridian newspaper, take you on a journey through tales that fit everywhere between Type O positive and Type AB negative. With a kickin' cover by Laura Givens and detailed illustrations by Marge Simon, *Blood Sampler* is a must-read even if you don't care for the suckers.

Type: Anthology – vampire – flash fiction

Ordering Link:

https://www.hiraethsffh.com/product-page/blood-sampler-by-david-lee-summers-lee-clark-zumpe

Survival and Sorcery

David Lee Summers

There is a saying: "Only the rocks live forever."

Scientists say that isn't actually true. I wonder if I will outlive the rocks. Some days the prospect quickens me. Other days it disturbs me.

My name is Sani Mendez and I have lived on a plot of land in northwestern New Mexico since the 1800s. My parents told me about white men when I was young, but I did not see one until railroad workers came in 1880 to build a line for the Atlantic and Pacific railroad. All of us in the lands of the Diné knew our lives wouldn't be the same. More men came through and created a town they called Gallup. It attracted all kinds of people seeking new opportunities. It also attracted a vampire seeking fresh hunting grounds.

The vampire attacked me while I was out by the sheep pen early one evening, feeding the flock. He didn't expect a simple shepherd to fight back, but I did. He grabbed me from behind, pinned one of my arms and drove his fangs into my neck. With my free arm, I retrieved a knife from my belt and drove it into his side. He reared back and stumbled over his feet in his haste to flee. I saw him as a monster, or perhaps a witch. I jumped on him and stabbed him in the neck. The blood from his jugular sprayed on me and into my mouth.

He pushed me off him and disappeared into the night. I fell onto the ground, licked my lips and swallowed. At that time, I didn't know what exactly had happened. I guessed he'd injured me worse than I thought. As far as I could tell, I lay there, dying.

I awoke with a start, later that night as my father looked over me. He asked me what had happened and I told him. He said he thought a skinwalker must have attacked me. He pointed to footprints leading away from me. The human footprints turned into those of an animal. At that moment, I realized my throat no longer hurt. I clambered to my feet and looked. The animal tracks resembled those of a wolf. Maybe the creature had been a skinwalker after all.

Just then, insatiable hunger came over me. I probed the inside of my mouth with my tongue and discovered fangs. I thought perhaps the skinwalker had turned me into one of its kind. I knew if I remained, I may not have control over my appetites, so I ran far and fast, my dad's voice echoing behind me.

I don't know how far I ran, but I eventually reached a field with cattle. I surprised myself by grabbing a cow and wrestling her to the ground. I bit into her neck and drank. I killed that cow and her blood sustained me, but I had no desire to drink from another. My stomach cramped, like after a feast day when I'd eaten too much at one sitting.

Late that night, I returned home, but I felt ashamed. I couldn't face my parents. I sneaked into our hogan while they slept, grabbed some clothes and then sought shelter. While in the hogan, I thought I heard my parents whispering to one another despite their gentle snores. I soon realized their thoughts seeped into my brain. I sensed their worry. I tried to reassure them I would be fine. As I did, my father stirred and I knew the time had come to leave.

I knew of a cave not far away where I sometimes hid from the monsoon rains in late summer. Late the next afternoon, the sunlight crept into the cave, burning my arm. I fled deeper into the cave. That night, I tried to understand what I had become. I willed myself to transform into a wolf or a coyote, but nothing happened. I realized I must not be a skinwalker, after all.

Still, I had already gained some understanding of my newfound abilities. I knew I had great strength and I could sense thoughts. I knew I hungered. I made my way to Fort Wingate, where soldiers kept watch over us Indians. I found a soldier patrolling the perimeter, subdued him easily and drank his blood. I didn't make the mistake of the vampire who made me. I didn't let the guard keep a free hand to retrieve any sidearms. Although the soldier possessed less blood than the cow, it proved far more satisfying.

Whatever I was, I realized I was a man with great power and few limitations. I made my way to Santa Fe, a town big enough to sustain me. The problem was, I discovered that bigger cities have disadvantages as well. I may have been a powerful Navajo, but I was no match for a group of ordinary mortals.

They decided to seek me out one day after I took blood from a hooker several men liked. Fortunately, they sought me out immediately during the night. I could still move about and react to them. They shot me with ordinary lead and left me for dead. I awoke in great pain just before the sunrise and made my way to a hiding place. I decided to keep a low profile from then on.

I never quite knew what I was until 1900 when a novel called *Dracula* turned up in a Santa Fe bookshop. I read the description of the vampire and realized I must be one of Dracula's kindred.

I didn't meet another vampire until World War II. That's when Desmond Drake recruited me to help him during the war in the Pacific. "I need someone who speaks the language of the Diné, so I can know American troop movements and keep them safe."

I agreed and, for the first time in my immortal life, I was paid a generous salary. Of course, I couldn't help but appreciate that I myself was now a union soldier like the one I fed on early in my immortal existence.

In that time, the town called Gallup grew up near my family's land. It was a railroad stop for many years, then a stop on Route 66. After I returned home from the Pacific, I decided I missed that part of the world. My parents were long gone and I found their hogan abandoned. I fixed it up as best I could and took possession of the land.

Two decades later, I replaced the hogan with a mobile home. I found it easier to keep daylight from encroaching while I slept. I maintained a low profile over the years, only going into Gallup occasionally to feed. Other Diné tended to avoid me, thinking I must be some kind of witch. That disappointed me, because I missed the company of my people, but I understood.

Little of consequence happened over the years until a couple of months ago, when a coyote showed up on my land. I tried to shoo it away, but it spoke to me.

"You're an acquaintance of Desmond Drake, are you not?" asked the Coyote.

I narrowed my gaze. "I worked for him almost 70 years ago," I said.

"He needs your help." The coyote explained that he was one of the Yei, one of the spirit beings my people revere.

I blinked at the animal. "Drake is a powerful vampire. How can I help him?"

"Let me show you." The coyote took me to his world, a place that put the cities of the white people to shame. Crystalline buildings were interspersed among beautiful gardens of flowers unlike any I had ever seen before. Coyote explained that American soldiers may try to take this place for their own if they weren't stopped. I could help prevent that if I helped Drake again. Coyote suggested that I might learn to visit this place on my own some day and I would be welcome anytime I wanted to visit.

He didn't need to say much more to persuade me. I let him take me to Los Alamos to help Drake defeat the scientists who would control a beautiful world far away. After we defeated the scientists, Drake helped me get transportation back home to Gallup. And so I find myself back home on my land on a quiet night.

I stepped outside to enjoy the stars, but happened to look down. There, on my porch, lay a witchcraft bundle.

* * *

What I found was a small leather bag containing numerous items. I'd seen medicine bundles before. The items in this one weren't those a medicine man or woman would carry. We Diné don't discuss forbidden items. Even though I am a vampire, I respect our people's traditions and I recognized items in this bundle that made me shiver.

As I say, back when I was first attacked, I thought the creature that had attacked me was a skinwalker. Over the decades, other Diné have also assumed that I am a skinwalker. I wondered if this bundle had been dropped on my doorstep as a warning of sorts. Still, this seemed an odd warning. Most Diné I knew wouldn't collect the items I found in this bag. I suspected I had been visited by a sorcerer.

I took the bundle inside and lay the items out on my dining room table. I looked for clues about where I might find the sorcerer who left this. I frowned as I examined the contents. Everything inside was easily available all around the northwestern corner of New Mexico and well into Arizona.

I tapped my fingers on the table and considered what to do. I didn't think the person who left the bundle left it as a warning. I suspected they dropped it accidentally. If that were the case, they'd be back for it. The problem was, I had no guarantee they'd be back when I was awake.

I packed everything back into the leather pouch and considered it. I actually had a similar pouch that I'd purchased a few years ago. I grabbed it from a drawer and lay it next to the other. Side by side, I could easily see the differences, but at a distance, they would be hard to tell apart.

I decided the way to find the sorcerer who dropped the witchcraft bundle would be to take a page from Desmond

Drake's playbook. I left my leather pouch on a table by my couch in the living room and left the lamp on. Stepping outside, I looked through the window. Sure enough, I could see it. From that distance, I doubted even the owner of the witchcraft bundle could tell it wasn't his—or hers. When a white person hears the word "witch" they tend to assume a woman. When a Navajo hears the word, they often assume a man. Neither one is right. In my experience, magic tempts all genders equally.

I took the real witchcraft bundle with me, locked the door, and drove into Gallup. At the Walmart, I purchased a camera and a motion-detection system with an alarm. After shopping, I took some time to hunt near the shops where white men sold Native "curios" to tourists.

When I returned home, I found my front door kicked in. The fake witchcraft bundle sat on the floor near an opposite wall. I guessed the intruder had grabbed it, discovered it wasn't what they wanted, and hurled it away. They had opened up drawers around the house and turned them out. I wished the intruder had taken the time to neaten up after themselves. They only got to around half the drawers in my mobile home, so some noise must have startled them away.

Flush with recent blood, I spent the rest of the night installing the motion detectors and a couple of cameras, then neatened up my house as best as I could. Unfortunately, the sorcerer had broken my lock, but I had a spare doorknob. By the time I'd replaced that, the first rays of twilight brightened the eastern sky.

I went into my bedroom, pulled down the blackout blinds and fell asleep.

The alarm awoke me late the next afternoon. I woggled the mouse on my computer to wake it up. I hoped it wouldn't prove to be some neighbor's dog snooping around. Fortunately, it did prove to be a man. He was being cautious, now that my pickup had returned. He peered in low windows. It was still bright enough outside that I couldn't go out and catch him, or even call to him.

I reached out with my mind. Whoever this person was, they didn't guard their thoughts. Apparently, telepathy isn't part of a sorcerer's playbook. I caught a very traditional name, Tsela Nez. The first name meant "stars lying down." I smiled; it seemed a good name for someone who opposed a vampire.

As I continued to probe, I gathered my intruder was a young person and they didn't live very far away. Still, the young man didn't want to wander too far and lose their opportunity to retrieve the medicine bundle. They stalked off to some rocks near my trailer and resolved to wait for me to make an appearance. Those rocks afforded them a good view of my front door.

I lay back down on my bed and closed my eyes. It was late enough in the afternoon, I didn't fall back to sleep, but I rested until the sunset. Once the sun went down, I stepped outside. I held up the witchcraft bundle.

"Tsela Nez," I called. "Is this what you want?"

Something snarled from behind the rocks. I stepped down from my porch and continued to listen. A tall, wolf-like creature sprung from behind the rocks. As it ran toward me, I took a careful look. It wasn't exactly a wolf. It still maintained a basically human-shaped body, but had a wolf's head and ears. It wore a traditional belt and jewelry. It launched itself at me and tackled me. It reached for the witchcraft bundle I held, but I grasped it tight.

I shoved the creature and forced it onto its back. I opened my mouth and latched onto the creature's furry throat. For a moment, my memories carried me back to that first time I drank blood from a cow.

The creature yelped as I drank its blood. I gained a much clearer picture of the creature's background. This was Tsela Nez, a young sorcerer. He led a group of other young men and women interested in traditional witchcraft. He came snooping around when he'd heard rumors of the old skinwalker in the area. I released him and he scuttled backwards. I tossed the witchcraft bundle at him. He grabbed it from the air.

He then turned and ran. As he did, a glow surrounded his body and bubble-like nimbus enveloped him. The bubble shot off into the night, much faster than a man could run. I thought that looked like a handy trick.

The blood of this skinwalker invigorated me. I went inside and brought up my web browser. It was time to figure out where this Tsela Nez actually lived. That bubble trick reminded me of things I'd seen on Coyote's world and I thought it might pay to learn more about it.

* * *

Tsela Nez lived about twenty miles away from me. On Navajo land, that's practically next door. I climbed in my pickup and drove to his place. He lived on land with a mobile home smaller than mine, next to an old hogan. I guessed he actually lived in the mobile home. Hogans can be rather comfortable, but they can also be challenging to maintain. I knocked on the trailer's door.

Nez surprised me by appearing at the hogan's door. "What do you want?"

He didn't realize I knew what he looked like in human form. Still, I sensed a certain nervousness from him. What's more, he now knew I wasn't exactly human. "I have tasted your blood. I have seen inside your mind. I know you are yee naaldlooshii, one who goes on all fours, a skinwalker."

He narrowed his gaze. "All right, so you know. That doesn't answer my question, what do you want from me?"

I shrugged. "I want to know why you were on my land, snooping around. I keep to myself. I don't meddle in your affairs."

He folded his arms. "Meddling takes many forms. Some in this area say you are yee naaldlooshii. One seeks this gift as a way of gaining mastery over nature. I will abide no competition. If you aren't my ally, you must be my enemy."

"I have lived a very long time." I chanced a step closer to him. "I do not seek mastery over nature. I just wish to live in peace."

"If you are not a skinwalker, then what are you? You drink blood and talk of seeing into my mind. That is sorcery."

I snorted. "I have come to learn it's something humans call nanotechnology, a legacy left by meddling yei many centuries ago. The chemicals in my cells have altered me so that I must subsist on blood. I can see and hear better than most people. I can run farther and faster than ordinary humans. I can sense the electromagnetic impulses of the human brain and translate them into language. I can also transform into an animal, but it is not as terrifying as the one you transform into." I held out my hands and disappeared into the fabric of space itself. Even as I did, fur bristled out over my arms. A long tail sprouted from my backside. My ears became pointed and shifted to the top of my head.

At once, I existed outside the universe and within the mind of a small animal staring at Nez with wide, green eyes. He gasped and took a step back in spite of himself. Then he smiled and knelt down before me. "You can become a ringtail." He shook his head. "You are a ringtail in entirety. That is powerful sorcery indeed." He didn't volunteer to show me his sorcery.

I hissed at him and he took another step backward. As he did, I reverted to my human form. "You do not transform completely, like I do. You are still partly human."

He remained silent for a long time. He turned his back and I thought he would go into the hogan and close the door without telling me anything more. Just as he reached the threshold, he gestured to me. "Is that sufficient invitation to one of your kind?"

I barked a laugh. "Not all the stories about vampires are accurate."

He led me into his hogan. Open windows let in outside light. He sat down at a table and gestured to the seat across from him. "When you transform, do you actually reduce your mass and become a little ringtail, or do you exchange places with a ringtail from somewhere else?"

I considered that. The process of transformation always seemed like a little of both. "I suppose it's more of an exchange than a true transformation."

He pursed his lips and nodded. "It's the same with us. We learn to summon the beast." He pointed to his chest. "It is at once within us and somewhere else."

"Ringtails are not hard to find in New Mexico, where do you find the . . ." I tried to find the right words, ". . . the creature you become."

"The cosmos . . . the multiverse, if you will . . . is vast. There are realms much like ours and realms much different. There are worlds much like ours and realms much different. We may be called yee naaldlooshii, but we do not crawl on all fours. We fly." He snapped his fingers and all at once a glowing orb surrounded Tsela Nez. The orb winked out and he had vanished. A moment later, Nez opened the hogan's door and entered. "Sorcery is power. It's power to walk between the world of dreams and the real world."

I snorted a laugh. "You sound like you've been reading Carlos Castaneda."

Nez shrugged. "You have a point. Dude did too much peyote, but he came close to touching truths about the structure of the universe."

"The orb you generated . . . what is it, exactly?"

He remained silent.

"A few weeks ago, I traveled through space in a similar way using the magic of the yei. I believe they created a dimensional corridor that let us move quickly from one point in space to another. Is your orb something similar?"

I referred to the way Coyote transported me to his home world.

"The orbs are like bubbles in the fabric of space. Once you know how to form them, they're easy."

"Can you teach me?"

He narrowed his gaze. "What can I teach an old vampire like you?"

"How to summon the orbs. How you became yee naaldlooshii."

"There are rituals." He walked back to the table and dropped into the chair facing me. "Perhaps you have glimpsed the science behind the rituals. There is power in understanding how the magic works. If I teach you the rituals, will you promise to help me understand what the magic is doing?"

"I'm willing to do my best." I leaned forward. "Vampires and yee naaldlooshii have lived in the shadows for much too long. What is the good of power if we cannot wield it to improve our lot?" I looked around at the hogan.

Nez considered that. "I've seen your home and I've glimpsed your powers. I did not think material gain was your priority."

"It isn't," I admitted, "but I'd be glad to be able to travel where I would without being hemmed in by this reservation and without being constrained by limited finances."

"In that way, we are much alike." He reached out and took my hand. I reveled in its warmth and the pulse of blood flowing through his veins.

Movie review: Nanny
Lee Clark Zumpe

There may be as many definitions of the phrase "American dream" as there are Americans. The etymology of the term shows that its meaning has evolved over the decades. Thank American writer and historian James Truslow Adams for popularizing the phrase in the 1931 book "The Epic of America." Adams wrote that "life should be better and richer and fuller for everyone, with opportunity for each according to ability or achievement." Adams goes on to say that the American dream "is not a dream of motor cars and high wages merely, but a dream of social order in which each man and each woman shall be able to attain to the fullest stature of which they are innately capable, and be recognized by others for what they are, regardless of the fortuitous circumstances of birth or position."

That assertion echoes tenets affirmed in the Declaration of Independence: that we are created equal and that we are born with the right to "Life, Liberty and the pursuit of Happiness."

Politicians like to bend the meaning of the phrase to suit their agenda.

In his 1965 State of the Union address, Lyndon B. Johnson remarked that "Our own freedom and growth have never been the final goal of the American dream. We were never meant to be an oasis of liberty and abundance in a worldwide desert of disappointed dreams. Our nation was created to help strike away the chains of ignorance and misery and tyranny wherever they keep man less than God means him to be."

Richard Milhous Nixon, in his first inaugural address in 1969, said that "the American dream does not come to those who fall asleep" as he sought to reform the welfare system. In 1977, Jimmy Carter told listeners that "the American dream endures. We must once again have full faith in our country — and in one another. I believe

America can be better." In 1997, Bill Clinton said that "Martin Luther King's dream was the American dream. His quest is our quest: the ceaseless striving to live out our true creed."

Barack Obama, in his 2014 State of the Union address, admitted that his "opportunity agenda won't be complete, and too many young people entering the workforce today will see the American dream as an empty promise, unless we also do more to make sure our economy honors the dignity of work and hard work pays off for every single American."

Though the American dream was not originally intended to encourage the accumulation of individual wealth, some see it as mantra for unbridled, aggressive capitalism — a rallying cry to those who place self above society.

Many people immigrate to the United States in search of the increasingly elusive American dream. Despite the hardship of leaving home and family behind, they believe they will find more promising opportunities in America — better jobs, better living conditions, better education, and in some cases, to escape hostile conditions in their own country.

In the new horror film "Nanny," Aisha (Anna Diop) views America as her best chance at building a better life for herself and her young son. "Nanny" was written and directed by Nikyatu Jusu. The Amazon Studios film found its way into select theaters in late November before being released to streaming Dec. 16, 2022, on Prime Video.

Aisha — an undocumented immigrant living in New York City — comes to the United States from the West African country of Senegal. Staying with a family member, she finds a job as a nanny working for a privileged couple in an expensive apartment. She is eager to earn enough money to bring her 6-year-old son and her cousin to America.

It is evident from the beginning that being separate from her child is causing Aisha significant hardship. Though she trusts her Senegalese family to watch over him in her absence, she is overwhelmed by guilt that intensifies each day as she struggles to raise the funds she needs to guarantee their reunion. That task becomes increasingly difficult as her employers — Amy (Michelle Monaghan) and Adam (Morgan Spector) — are so self-absorbed that they make her caretaker gig a grating experience. If they weren't wealthy, Amy and Adam would likely be found guilty of child neglect. Their wealth makes them incapable of maintaining any form of customary social relationship. Their affection for each other — and for their child, Rose (Rose Decker) — is flimsy façade.

Unsurprisingly, they treat Aisha as little more than a piece of property they have acquired. They exploit her kindness. Jusu taps into a racial caricature here that may not conform visually to the stereotype but certainly evokes it in terms of how the husband and wife view their domestic servant. Aisha challenges their preconceived notions, however, demanding they pay her what she is owed according to the arrangement they made. She also does not allow either parent to denigrate or demean her.

As she is dealing with these issues, Aisha finds herself beset by disturbing visions and nightmares. The viewer is left questioning Aisha's sanity as elements of African folklore overlap precursors of depression and grief.

"Nanny" meanders clumsily through aesthetically pleasing scenes with a dreamy inertia that impedes to fully connect with the main character. Aisha is featured in nearly every scene: You would be hard-pressed to find more than 30 seconds of this film in which Diop is not on screen. We may empathize with her plight, but the script keeps her isolated and inaccessible.

"Nanny" is best described as engaging arthouse horror. Its deliberate abstruseness is distracting. The narrative is choppy and sometimes lacks cohesion. It makes up for these deficiencies with a strong lead performance by Diop and with its overriding sense of ominous portent.

Many of the film's horror components have been plucked from the mainstream genre template, with obvious prompts from "The Nightmare on Elm Street" and "Rosemary's Baby." Other aspects of the film are reminiscent of Jordan Peele's "Go" and Reme Weekes' "His House." That is not to say that "Nanny" is derivative — Jusu simply taps into archetypes and prevalent motifs to establish a dark and surreal setting with indistinct boundaries. The viewer questions what is real and what is imagined.

The overall effect is more disquieting than frightening. "Nanny" isn't the kind of horror film that tries to shock its audience every 10 minutes with jump-scares and gross-outs. It wants to unsettle viewers — and to encourage them to think about things like social classes, racial inequity, and disparities in immigrant populations. It takes "Nanny" a very long time to get where it's going — and once it gets there, it feels like too much is left unresolved or forgotten. That ambiguity may be Jusu's way of challenging us to ponder our own definition of the American dream.

INFO BOX
"Nanny"
Genre: Psychological horror
Director: Nikyatu Jusu
Cast: Anna Diop, Michelle Monaghan, Sinqua Walls, Morgan Spector, Rose Decker, and Leslie Uggams
Release date: Nov. 23, 2022
Run time: 98 minutes
Rated: R

Lost Dreams Bookshop

By James W. Bullard

The old bookshop has been around before people can remember. An aging caretaker is finally being replaced and the new manager realizes the shop itself is sentient. The bookshop survives by deriving energy from its patron's lost dreams and uses that energy to manipulate people. A series of barely interacting victims who have shopped in the store over the years are telepathically summoned to return to the shop and gather on a single day not realizing their fate is in the hands of the sentient shop.

James W. Bullard lives in Colorado with his girlfriend, his son, and a spoiled Aussie shepherd. Writing is a hobby along with watercolor painting and drinking craft beer.

Type: Novella
Audience: adults

Ordering Links:
Print Edition ($10.95):
https://www.hiraethsffh.com/product-page/lost-bookshop-by-james-w-bullard
ePub Edition ($3.99):
https://www.hiraethsffh.com/product-page/lost-dreams-bookshop-by-james-w-bullard
PDF Edition ($3.99):
https://www.hiraethsffh.com/product-page/lost-dreams-bookstore-by-james-w-bullard

Quantum Poetry
James Bullard

Cold winds swirled dead leaves across the hard paver stones in front of the library steps. Gray clouds overhead further muted the drab colors of a winter world and cast a somber mood over shivering pedestrians that rushed from one warm place to another. Misshapen forms waddled along the sidewalk in down-stuffed jackets, layers of insulated pants, puffy mittens, plastic boots, and heavy wool stocking caps. Inside the library, a respite from the uncomfortable temperatures outside awaited. A welcome waystation from this dreary day, an open invitation to explore possibilities of escaping this monotony, this wasted time, this frozen season, this dull life.

To pass the lunch hour away from responsibilities seemed like a much-needed break in the middle of a cold workday for many people. The golden light escaping the glass doors whispered a silent seduction to those who wandered close and enticed all into her invisible grasp. Come inside, the books beckoned. Warm your fingers on our pages. Fill your mind with fires of truth, lies, and fantasy.

I heeded the call, lured by the visual siren song to enter through the double doors. My eyes closed as the blast of heated air rushed against me. Was I a victim of mystic hypnosis? Hardly. I'd ventured here many times to be free of the maddening world. I relished this addiction. This quiet, consistent other place enjoyed my company, stirred my curiosity, broadened my scope of reality, and lulled me into a half-hypnotized half energized prodigious reader. The self-inflicted education was a sustenance to motivate me. I constantly craved the exploration of

47

something new, challenging, and life-altering. Often, I lost track of reality and time and spent far more than my allotted lunch hour buried in works of fiction, biographies, or tales of the macabre. I wandered the aisles to inspire fantasies of sleuthing unsolved cases, to discover unknown civilizations, or merely to stumble upon a revelation to an unasked question. The library hummed with a peculiar silence that displaced the constant tinnitus ringing in my ears. My overstimulated brain relaxed while I strolled between shelves, picked out an interesting title, and settled into a polished wooden cubicle to devour a few chapters before sighing deeply as my free time expired.

I wasn't alone in my bliss. Others were here to read, search, or just soak in the heat because they had none of their own. The cubicle was my sanctuary. Its high panels blocked distractions like blinders to ignore the shuffling feet that circled the halls. My eyes focused on the words, sentence after sentence lined up on the crisp vanilla creme pages. My ears muffled any stray voices with a constant overtone of a far-off jet engine of the library air exchanger. I held my breath when a waft of unwashed, sweaty human stench invaded my nose. My fingers lovingly caressed the smooth, creaseless pages, the solid cover slick with glossy artwork, a real thing to touch that confirmed its existence without effort.

I was on an island surrounded by personal space. Rare was the disturbance that caused my eyes to diverge from the page. Rare was the irritation at the barely audible voice, the hushed whispers of docents guiding patrons to obscure titles on high shelves, and the sudden laughter and giggles of children. There was a reverence for the peace of this space kept by almost all who worshiped here. Nearly all who ventured into these solemn halls to worship the written page did so alone. A solitary endeavor unencumbered by the opinions of others allowed for curiosity to guide the search for whatever the mind desired.

I paid little attention to every lone wanderer who passed through my zone of senses. But I paused to sneak a casual glance at a young couple who tried to look inconspicuous as they held hands and slowly strolled through the library not looking for anything in particular. I sensed the nervous energy exchanged between them and saw their eyes glimmer as they smiled at each other. They disappeared behind a tall row of reference volumes and made no attempt to hide the sound of their fevered kisses. It was easy to imagine hearts racing as they let loose passions, attempted to be sneaky with their lust, and indulged a curiosity, the curve of heaving breasts, an aroused nipple, and a bulged front pocket as they tasted sighs and tongues. They looked old enough to know the inappropriateness of their public affection but I wondered if they were hiding more than just kisses, hiding identities in obscure corners. A mask of anonymity tends to make us brave. No one knows us. No one cares. We all have secrets. Who was I to judge? I returned to my quiet isolation, my other place, my current read. The scene left an imprint subconsciously, a little kernel of want, a dust mote of envy. I tried to ignore it and let it settle somewhere dark. Reality often left a bad taste but was quickly washed away by reading any chapter of fantasy.

My hour-long break from the day had come and gone. Obligations returned to my mind in a sudden rush of stress. Reluctantly, I closed the incredible Lovecraft novel, marked the chapter with a treasured bookmark, and let it slowly fade into a sweet memory. I took a deep breath in an attempt to recharge but remained glued to my chair, safe in my self-imposed quarantine. I wanted to stay in this quiet place instead of returning to the maddening pace of unfulfilling work. I contemplated fading into the background of some obscure fantasy story, becoming a forgotten character in a sci-fi world. Often, I longed to be a part of an imaginary realm rather than in this real one. In this world, I was a speed bump in everyone else's journey.

Then, I heard the muffled voices drift over my cubicle wall. I questioned if the conversation existed only in my head. Deep, grumbling tones were tossing disagreeable jabs back and forth, and an argument between two wise old bears brought an image into my head that put a smile on my face. Had sentient wildlife infiltrated the quiet library? Were furry monsters engaged in a debate about the importance of physicists in the history of the world? I gathered my effects and tiptoed toward the growling that barely registered more than a whisper. I spied the source of the sound at the far end of a shelf full of biographies. Somewhat disappointed to see two older men in tattered clothes and not grizzlies, I sighed and stifled a laugh. But the conversation held my interest enough that I wandered in their direction, feigning interest in old presidents lined up on the shelves.

"You are thinking about the wrong Proust. The physicist Proust didn't write Swann's way. He established the definite proportions theorem. Einstein used this basis to come up with his relativity."

"Maybe you're right. My knowledge of Earth's history is a bit fuzzy. But why is the poetic Proust the trigger when next to Einstein's works? You realize that had Einstein not published his theorems, they could be enjoying a peaceful steam age instead of facing annihilation in the atomic."

"It's all academic at this point. Why does it matter, anyway? The coincidence opens the door. We can be off again without a trace. Have you had enough of this planet? The next stop will have much easier prey. I promise."

"I suppose. Nasty business, though. It's as if people didn't believe, total shock when faced with the inevitable."

"Yes, quite. The price of immortality. Someone has to pay. But no one will even remember their names."

I had to remind myself of the old adage not to judge a book by its cover. Both men had distinguished voices filtered through thick mustaches and beards that gave them a bit of credibility. Yet they both wore worn stocking caps over layers of gray and white stringy hair which draped over their shoulders in greasy layers. Their overcoats were dull brown wool with discolored patches on the upturned collars and down at the elbows. Similar faded brown wool pants and marred black leather shoes rose up over their ankles and wrinkled their pant hems. Their attire blended them into the background of the residentially challenged who passed their time wandering the library halls. They had the same height and build, one had brown eyes under bushy white eyebrows, and the other had blue eyes behind half-rimmed glasses. To give them a second glance would be a waste of effort. I made a snap judgment that they were vagrants and half expected their solemn request for a dollar for coffee if they caught me looking their way. They were only a part of the numerous homeless wanderers who meandered inside the library on a cold day to warm themselves only to be shooed away by the docent or security at closing time.

Their conversation quieted suddenly. They saw me straining to listen to them. The spectacled bear softly cleared his throat as he looked in my direction. I glanced up, flushed with embarrassment, and flashed a quick grin of apology as I turned back to the shelf to scan Dewey decimal numbers absentmindedly. I heard their shuffling steps patter around the end cap to the next aisle. Their grumbles resumed.

"The getting is good here. We can drop in on the next loop. Maybe stay a few days to explore the tastier places."

"Alright. But I believe we're attracting attention. We should go. Move on to the next intersection."

"Yes. Um. Was it this row or the last? By the big windows wasn't it?"

Their voices filtered between the rows of books so clearly from the other side of the rack as if they wanted me to hear the vague yet ominous declarations. My curiosity rose exponentially and fed my cravings for alternate realities. I pondered the idea that I could delve into this mystery of intelligent gents dressed in rags and ignore my responsibilities for a little while just to witness the insanity that had infected their minds and sent them on this path of delusion. Quickly, their voices trailed off into the darker corners of the endless aisles. I had to make a decision. My mind split. Should I follow them or put the episode behind me and return to work? But this incident was too bizarre to let pass by, too fantastic to ignore. The impossibility of these two characters slovenly dressed and speaking as if Earth wasn't from where they came was just too fascinating. It was as if this scenario had been written for a sci-fi novel from the 1950s. I felt I could spend a few more minutes dedicated to the investigation. No one would miss me at the office.

I started my search passively and looked with sideways glances down each aisle as I casually strolled deep into the unknown volumes. Solo readers stood quietly frozen in time. Their gazes fixed on the pale pages. Motionless eyes scanned for that tidbit of information or the solution to a problem hidden in their minds. The silence became eerie as no one talked or even breathed. The air thickened around me. The sound of the giant air exchanger with its constant repeating thump faded into nothing. My steps continued forward through an invisible fog. A force from nowhere started to push against me like winds in a storm. My brows furrowed, eyes squinted in concentration to move forward, to prevail against the restriction that wanted me to turn away from dark secrets.

I stumbled when the force abated suddenly, taking two wobbly steps forward to catch myself. Then I felt a gust of wind behind me rushing passed in silence. I imagined a spaceship had suddenly lost pressure from an explosion that opened the bulkhead and sucked every loose object into the vast darkness of endless space. My search took me to the last aisle of biographies of dead artists against the wall of windows that looked out into the downtown skyline. Snow had started falling outside, heavy flakes that blocked the view completely, a white veil in motion, swaying from endless gusts to dizzying effect. I glanced down the aisle and prepared to discover the two gents. Where else could they be? But they were gone. Vanished or perhaps hidden in the dim shadows at the end of the row. The air still buffeted at my back, a ghostly escort that guided my wandering further into the unknown. Cautiously, I stepped forward, checking over my shoulder for a surprise attack. A wave of apprehension sent a shiver down my spine as I neared the end of the aisle. I became aware of a flickering light that illuminated the middle of the rack. I pondered why someone lit a candle on the bookshelf. As I crept closer, those grumbling voices found their way to my ears again from somewhere distant. The winds at my back slacked a bit but still blew darkness around me. Then, I was surrounded by black except for the candlelight, just a pinpoint far away that grew in brightness and floated in the middle of the books. The circle of illumination grew to a brilliant glare and blocked the books from view. I shielded my eyes as my pupils tightened and then dared a peek.

Surely, my eyes had played a trick on my brain. There before me, an archway opened, carved through the books and metal shelves. The air swirled into this impossible portal, a breach in reality with flickering candlelight within the illusion. The arched passageway led to the interior of a room with a glossy hardwood floor and emerald-green walls brightened by a roaring fire in a brick fireplace. I blinked and shook my head in disbelief. As I focused my view in the dim space, I could see a large dining table surrounded by Queen-Anne chairs upholstered in purple velvet. The table was set with shining silver plates and a grandiose tea set with a multi-tiered pastry display. Candelabrum with stark white candles was burning brightly. A window beside the fireplace framed a gleaming sliver of a crescent moon. I turned around to look through the archway to the library windows behind me and saw the midday sun shining down on an icy sidewalk. Confused, I could not understand how the weather had changed so quickly. Then I heard the gentlemen conversing again, one barking orders for more tea to someone named Renfield. I turned back to gaze into the flickering candlelight.

I could not see anyone in the dining room. Voices floated to me from outside my view as I stood dumbfounded in the arched doorway. Suddenly, a swinging door opened in the far corner of the room. A man in a tuxedo barged in carrying a teapot on a silver tray. He stopped short but not because he saw me. His mouth gaped a moment before he cleared his throat to divert attention to where his eyes had fixed. At the far end of the dining table, the limp arm of a debonair man in a black smoking jacket slid slowly across the table pulled by the rest of the man's body as it dropped from the elaborate velvet chair to the hardwood floor. A trail of bright red liquid was left behind on the inlaid wood that could only be blood. It pooled where the wrist had been and left a trail where the arm dragged off the table. Candlelight flickered reflections in the glossy red gore streaked by lifeless fingers.

I couldn't help the exclamation that erupted, "Holy Shit!" I started to back away through the impossible doorway. Had I walked into a murder scene? Was I in danger myself from those two homeless gents? Before I could attempt a retreat, I heard a growling admonition directed toward the tuxedoed tea servant that echoed in the room.

"Renfield, you forgot to close the portal!" All eyes then darted on me, the apparition who didn't belong, the uninvited stranger crashing the tea party. My heart leaped into my throat and cinched around my airway. I closed my eyes and wished desperately that this was all a dream. In a blink, my heart sank to the pit of my stomach. My nerves went into flight or fight mode. I readied to run.

"Well, since you're here, sir, do come in." said a monstrously deep but welcoming voice near my ear. The portal closed behind me so silently that I backed into a darkly stained bookshelf set into the wall instead of an open door. I turned in a panic and groped at the leather-bound volumes along the shelves, searching frantically to find the missing door that had disappeared or never existed. I slumped my shoulders, dropped my head against the books, and waited for the assault I was sure to come.

"Have no fear, old chap. We mean you no harm," proclaimed one of the old men. His voice echoed low as in the library. His beard was different now, trimmed in a goatee. But he still wore the half-rimmed glasses. "Are you the odd duck who was stalking us in the library?"

"No, I," my voice squeaked to silence. I had lost my will to live and some much-needed motor functions. I was traumatized by the confusing scene. My back slid along the wall as I tried to distance myself from the now well-dressed grizzly bears. But there was nowhere to go. My eyes fixed on the pooled blood that initiated the streak left on the table that pointed to a horrible end. The whole scene felt staged. Memories of books I had read over the years flooded my mind. Detective novels starring Sherlock Holmes, Hercule Poirot, and even the Hardy Boys and Scooby-Doo mingled in a flurry of possibilities.

The other gentleman, whose long gray beard was now a bizarre fluffy black mutton chop, spoke up to offer tea to soothe my nervousness. Renfield was beardless but had a twitching mustache. He moved toward me with a silver cup of brown liquid in his outstretched hand. My instinct was to dodge and run, but there was no place to escape. With a deep sigh, I took the cup and inhaled the steam while my hand trembled and swirled the tea in a shaky spiral. I suspected poisoned tea, so I took a fake sip as Renfield backed away and slipped through the swinging door.

The man with the mutton chops smiled and introduced himself. "My name is Dr. Violet. This is my home. My associate is Mr. Holiday. That was Renfield, my manservant." He pointed toward the swinging door to no one. "The, uh, our unfortunate guest, as you can see, has taken his own life, it seems." He covered his nose with a white silk handkerchief. Turning his focus to Mr. Holiday, he said, "The smell of death is already upon him."

"Seems you have joined our party inadvertently," said Mr. Holiday as he addressed me, the wide-eyed wallflower in the room. "Perhaps you could introduce yourself?" His eyes glared at me. A quick judgment formed in his head. I was a suspect. I was an anomaly in this impossible nightmare. I intruded into a world unknown to me, a time and place that I'd never been. I wondered if I had inhaled some ancient book dust or a trace of meth left by an addict on a shelf in the library. The teacup felt solid in my hand. The scent of brewed leaves permeated the air while the liquid swirled around in a clockwise direction. This experience was real enough to provide sensations to my nerves, to fire the neurons in my brain. This was my reality and these strange characters were part of it.

I took a long draw from the teacup and then remembered it was probably poisoned. My eyes fluttered as I swallowed. I waited for the burn of some kind of life-ending pain. Nothing happened. I cleared my throat and attempted a proper introduction, "Hello, um, I'm, uh, my name is Crow." I hoped my wavering voice would not raise suspicion. I mentally kicked myself for using my real name. "I don't understand how it is that I'm here and not in the library. Where am I?" My voice cracked noticeably. My hand continued to shake the teacup.

Mr. Holiday took a step forward and puffed out his chest. His mustache had a perfect curl at both ends slicked with grease which suggested a sinister vibe. His eyeglasses shimmered in the candlelight as he spoke, "Libraries are temporal intersections, Mr. Crow. Those who understand the dynamics can use them to travel interdimensionally. He paused to judge my reaction and continued, "Dr. Violet and I are taking a tour of the universe using the infinite loop as our rail and Dr. Violet's distortion envelope as our carriage. On this circuit, we've paired up publications from Proust and Einstein. The results have been interesting, to say the least."

Dr. Violet had been examining the body on the floor. He stood holding his handkerchief over his nose and mouth. "Poor chap must have given up waiting for our return. Gone mad with grief and slashed his forearms from elbow to wrist. We had explained the terms to join us on our adventure. He readily agreed before we could even divulge the details. Renfield! Bring the wheelbarrow!"

"Who is he?" I asked already knowing that it didn't matter to me.

"Why that's none other than Albert Einstein himself," answered Dr. Violet rather smugly. "We found a portal to the Princeton library on a previous loop and invited him to travel with us to see his genius theory in action. I guess becoming undead did not appeal to him after all. But it's the only way to enjoy the loop. He was rather distraught back then but there weren't any options to return to his time. Traveling this way is exceedingly fast but the loop is infinitely long."

I stared at Dr. Violet's bright brown eyes and remembered them from the library. He was indeed the same vagrant I saw before. His clothes now looked very well-to-do and immaculately clean. His appearance had somewhat changed, but he was still the same man I saw arguing in the library aisle. Mr. Holiday, too, had taken on a younger appearance than at the library. His clothes had vastly improved as well. For whatever reason, my brain was calculating years as I admired their clothes. I ventured a question and posed it to both of them, "Einstein has been with you for . . . 68 years?"

"Yes. Hasn't aged a day. I'm rather surprised a genius would choose suicide over becoming a vampire. Perhaps his belief in God swayed him to pick the lesser of evils. Ha!" Dr. Violet chuckled and smiled wide enough to reveal dagger-like fangs polished to a sheen that glimmered in the candlelight. "But it was his suggestion to combine his published works and the works of a poet like Proust to open a new portal on Earth. We only happened to find the Princeton library back in 1955 by putting Homer next to Plato."

Mr. Holiday sighed deeply and stared at his teacup, "I genuinely wanted Mr. Einstein's life force to make me feel smarter. But now it's ruined. So sad."

My knees began to wobble as the questions tornadoed through my head and tipped me over to rest my hands on the solid table. Finally, words spilled out of my mouth at racing speed, "Wait! Vampires? You're vampires and this is some kind of spaceship? We're zipping through spacetime right now? How long have you been alive, I mean undead? Is that really Einstein? Didn't they miss him back then? Why wasn't that in the news? How can . . . wait? Am I on a YouTube gag? A hidden camera or something?" I laughed hysterically and then yelped when Renfield returned with a wooden wheelbarrow barging through the swinging door. Its single wheel squeaked on its ancient iron pin as it rolled across the hardwood planks.

Dr. Violet's glasses reflected a lone candle that flickered on the table as he turned to face me. "Mr. Crow . . . for all intents and purposes, this is your reality now. We will explain soon. At the moment, we need to dispose of the carnage of the professor before it stinks up the distortion bubble."

Renfield lifted Mr. Einstein by his underarms. Mr. Holiday assisted by gathering limp legs. Together, they wrangled the ungainly form into the bucket of the wheelbarrow. The tangle of white hair on Einstein's head somehow proved it really was him. Slabs of glossy red plastic peeled off the floor with the body as if his blood had congealed into a solid mass. Even the streaks on the table lifted with little effort like removing transparent tape. Mr. Holiday grumbled like the old bear I heard in the library as he daintily dropped the remnants into the wheelbarrow beside the body, his pinkie ajar. "Goes bad so quickly," he squirmed. But Renfield made no sounds and exerted little effort when he rolled the carcass away.

"Where . . . I mean . . . what will happen to him?" I asked more to derive an inkling as to my own fate.

"He'll become stardust once again. Nothing created and nothing lost. I think he'd like that. Back to the energy from whence he came. A simple transfer." Dr. Violet put his hand over his heart as if to honor the man and his mind.

"Is that what you'll do to me?" my voice quivered.

"If you choose that route. But I hope you would choose a chance of a lifetime and longer if you wish." Dr. Violet smiled at his joke and showed his fangs again. His demeanor reflected no malice towards me. I sensed a hint of relieved loneliness and fresh excitement with the introduction to someone new. "To be honest, Mr. Crow, I've lost track of the passage of time. I have no point of reference, no sun to circle to indicate years. I don't sleep. I was just a young cadet when I volunteered for this mission on my home world. The mission was a one-way trip because it was an experiment in black hole travel. I discovered the universe is endless because it is a loop. The loop is infinite. It reaches every galaxy, star system, and planet where intelligent life exists. So my library continues to grow." He pointed to the wall of bookshelves I had examined, frantically searching for a doorway. "I've collected from many different worlds and learned many different languages. The original mission was to discover portals along the event horizons. I don't fully understand the mechanics of this random connection between two disparate authors that generates a portal where I can step off the loop for a time and explore whatever world the portal opens for us. Access remains available as long as the book pair are coupled. Then we can return to the bubble and close the portal when the book pair is uncoupled. It truly is amazing. It's how I enjoy my existence, Mr. Crow, exploring the unknown. It's how I met Mr. Holiday, my blessed vampire. He offered me a way to continue my journey indefinitely. And it's been wonderful. I think Aristotle and Sophocles coupled together originally opened the door to old Europe."

"Dr. Violet popped out of the library shelves at my castle one night," piped up Mr. Holiday. "That was back in the 13th century before Vlad became popular. Instantly, I was enamored with this handsome magician who could travel through library shelves. His arrival was fortuitous because I needed a way to escape the, uh, pressures of my little town. My behaviors were so misunderstood back then." He smiled at Dr. Violet. "But now . . . Ah, the things we have seen. The tastes we've enjoyed."

I could sense their intimacy, a level beyond just traveling companions. They had shared some intense experiences that had bonded them, a deep codependence. Each offered a type of immortality to the other. Together, they could discover more about the universe than anyone. They could be gods. A wave of envy sent a shiver down my neck followed by a wave of repulsion. They shared a moment between themselves. The silence became awkward. So, I broke it. "What about Renfield? Is he a vampire too?"

"No, no. Renfield is a mechanical man. We found him some time ago in an abandoned science library on some forgotten world. There weren't any organic beings left when we popped through the portal. Just old skeletons crumbling to dust. Sad story, really. Poor Renfield just standing there blinking, waiting for requests. No, Renfield is useful but not a talkative chap. He makes a decent pot of tea and delicious pastries, however. Speaking of which . . . " Dr. Violet shouted toward the swinging door. "Renfield! Do we have any of those orange scones left?"

"Do have a seat, Mr. Crow. I'm sure your mind is reeling," Dr. Violet pointed to the empty chair where the late Albert had been seated. Reluctantly, I moved toward the plush purple antique and inspected it for remnants of death but found none. I slowly settled into the comfort of an old world.

"This table," I added an inflection to suggest a question, "It looks like something out of an old English manor house."

"I became a huge fan of Charles Dickens after reading some of his works. Renfield was able to reimagine the housewares quite well, don't you think?" Dr. Violet ran his hands over the smooth dark wood, caressing the inlaid parquet and then the multi-tiered pastry display.

Quietly, the swinging door popped open with Renfield gliding through, a silver tray leading the way piled high with golden pastries and an assortment of jams. He set the tray on the table and announced he would bring hot tea in a moment. Then he disappeared through the swinging door. His shoes never made a sound on the hardwood floor.

I blinked several times and turned to Dr. Violet, "What's in there?" I tilted my head toward the swinging door.

"Oh, just more mechanicals. Renfield takes care of it all now and keeps the bubble moving right along. I used to tinker with the programming, but the distortion envelope mostly flies. The basic principle is that we're traveling faster than light which stops time inside the bubble. We can travel great distances, but relative time continues. Even at these speeds, we can only circle the loop once every 68 Earth years. Sometimes we'll hop off and spend a week on a tropical planet. Sometimes just a day if the spot is dreary. But the craving for living blood is insatiable when it comes. If we've stopped somewhere and the scent is strong, we both can't resist. We go on a spree until suspicions rise too high. Then we bail."

"So you kill people?" I asked in my Sherlock Holmes mockery. I almost propped my hand under my chin to act like I was smoking a pipe.

"Guilty as charged. We do try to be discreet. Select the most anonymous. But finding a delicious flavor does make the experience delightful. Someone intelligent or passionate heightens the thrill." Mr. Holiday almost seemed proud of his debauchery. "I admit to using some mild hypnosis on the pretty people. Seduction is still a fascinating endeavor for me. I see it in their eyes, the glazed look of terrified willingness to submit, to be food for a greedy animal. I make no apologies for my soul. I am what I am. I find the psychology of intelligent people fascinating, how they often equate sensuality with sexuality. How even the slightest affection can trigger such an eager response to become intimate. Then that wide-eyed realization of a life fading away when they feel their skin pierced. It's such a jolt to my senses when they squirm."

Dr. Violet added, "Mr. Holiday does find the most interesting specimens to share. He does have a type though. Busty, curvaceous, and inebriated." They both laughed.

I turned away with an ick on my face then jumped when Renfield returned with a pot of tea, placing it on the table next to the pastries. The memory of streaked blood on the table came back to me. "So, am I just food then?" I asked neither of them in particular. I heard a slight giggle and then a hum. I resigned myself to knowing I had reached the end of my life. My curiosity doomed me. No amount of detective sleuthing would resolve this mystery in a 30-minute episode length. Ruh ro, Raggy. I racked my brain for any line of questioning that could extend my final breaths.

"No, Mr. Crow. Not at the moment, anyway. We had mostly satiated our hunger at the little drinking establishment near your library before your intrusion. Silly girl with a flirty laugh barely able to stand upright from the level of intoxication. Mr. Holiday and I got our fill before she realized what had happened. I doubt anyone will miss her. For now, Mr. Crow, you are our guest and a student of universal expeditionary travels." Dr. Violet attempted to soothe my sparking nerves by taking a mouthful of scone and a sip of tea.

I let out a nervous sigh, "Oh, ok. Thanks. So what about aliens? Do you drink their blood?" A flash of oddly shaped beings writhing in anguish while being drained of blue-green fluids played in my head.

Dr. Violet turned to Mr. Holiday with a grin then they both busted out laughing. Once they had their snort and guffaw, Dr. Violet put his hand on my shoulder and imparted some long-held wisdom, "Mr. Crow, there are no aliens. Every organic life form is alien to every other. Now, granted, the beings we've encountered have all had a written language and books, hence libraries which offered the ability of our little voyager to stop and enter their world when we can find the right combination of authors. It's intriguing that authors of different planets, even different galaxies can open portals light years away from their origin. And luckily, most of the worlds we have visited have had some type of fluid in their bodies that carry the life force we do so enjoy. The beings on your Earth are highly evolved but pale compared to other planets along the loop. (No offense, Mr. Holiday). Many intelligent beings feed on a life force of other intelligent beings all over the universe, we've discovered. The universe is mad with vampires."

Mr. Holiday looked far off into an invisible distance, "Remember that underwater lab with the tentacled researcher? Now that was some yum. So worth the bruises and welts."

I mouthed, "Wow," and they both cackled. I took a sip of tea which dribbled down my chin when my fingers trembled. Grabbing a black cloth napkin from the table I soaked up the spill on my jacket and realized my phone was still inside the breast pocket. I pulled it out and considered taking a video in secret. But as I looked around the scene, it only looked like a parlor in an old Sherlock Holmes movie. There was no way to prove I was inside a distortion bubble traveling faster than the speed of light to some far-distant alien library. No cell signal and no Wi-Fi, either. I took a selfie and added a note to look up the GPS coordinates to remind myself of this impossible delusion. Maybe I'd wake up in an alley behind a bar with puncture wounds in my neck. The selfie could be the only evidence of my previous night's activities.

"Relax, Mr. Crow. For now, just watch and learn. Take notes with your communication device. Explore with us for a while. You won't age in our little bubble. Maybe when we return to this side of the loop in 68 years, your Earth will remain as you left it." He chuckled knowingly. "If not, you could continue on this incredible journey. You are welcome to join us as a space vampire."

Dr. Violet made a compelling argument. He knew I was trapped with them and could suck me dry whenever he wanted. That was the reality of the situation. I had stumbled into their unfathomable life of galactic vampire travelers and was just a provision in their stores unless I joined them as a bloodsucker. There was no escape. My only course of action was to enhance my likeability so they

64

would enjoy my company and extend my life in hopes that in some long distant future, they would spare me the life of vampirism. I had already made up my mind. If a genius like Einstein chose to extinguish himself rather than feast on the life force of innocents, that was what I should do too. To prolong my demise, I engaged in conversations and offered my interpretations of poems and scientific literature as the gentlemen reminisced.

Renfield returned and topped off my tea cup with a deliciously scented Earl Gray. As he poured, I asked him in a whisper, "Do you know Asimov's rules of robotics?"

"Of course, sir. Dr. Violet has many volumes of Asimov," Renfield replied in a hushed tone. The teapot ceased to pour any liquid as he remained motionless close to me.

"Renfield, I need protection in accordance with the first rule," my voice grumbled a bit in hopes that the vampires didn't hear. They were busy recalling their favorite conquests.

"The rules are fiction, sir," Renfield retorted quietly and paused, "but I understand." He resumed his duties and filled Dr. Violet's and Mr. Holiday's cups with a steaming brew from whence I knew not. The gentleman sipped and continued to regale me with their follies of ravaging the innocent of the universe.

Renfield returned to my end of the massive table and paused with his back turned toward me. He nudged my shoulder to suggest I should look in the direction he faced. On the endless bookshelves on the bottom row close to me was a collection of nondescript black logbooks with no labels or titles on the spine. Renfield continued through the swinging door to the mysterious part of the bubble. I focused on the black leather volumes lined up inconspicuously. As the gentleman continued their trip down memory lane and enjoyed each other's recollections of devious pursuits, I pulled one of the logbooks from the shelf and turned it to the last entry.

Mica Silas (3rd orbit from H, He sun) Humanoid, high intellect, their blood is amazingly nourishing. We feasted for days and could not get enough. We drained every living soul on the tiny planet and wiped them out. Hopefully, this will satiate us for a few months. Remember to skip this portal in the next loop. Anne Rice and Neil Degrasse Tyson will forever be a dead planet.

Dr. Violet and Mr. Holiday had annihilated the whole planet. A species of intelligent life eradicated by the blood lust of two narcissistic vampires. They were indeed monsters of the historically diabolical kind. I looked back at the bookshelf, the endless row of identical logbooks keeping records of countless extinction events caused by two unscrupulous fiends. A sudden spark of super heroism ignited the idea that I should rid the universe of this continuing tragedy. The question was how. And then what was to become of me?

I replaced the logbook unseen and then resumed browsing the higher shelves, scanning the spines for titles familiar and alien. Mr. Holiday noticed my interest and suggested a tome called *The Shining* by Stephen King. He said it was classic demented Earth humanity and, paired with the Earth poet Sylvia Plath, opened a portal to a forest world full of sentient horticulture light years from Earth.

He turned back to Dr. Violet. They exchanged memories of the immense flowers that could swallow a person whole and the shrubbery that walked and roared. Everything they touched there filled them with a sense of looming death and self-destruction. And yet, their parasitic existence drained away the life force of those living plants and left them desiccated and dead.

"What's our next stop?" I asked. Neither of the gentlemen seemed to be too concerned about stopping or exploring unknown worlds now. Only by casual chance did they pair up a novel of science and poetry to see if a portal would open for them. Mr. Holiday scanned the bookshelf and pulled down a tattered book. Dust motes floated around it as he rifled through the yellowed paper pages.

"I think this is one of Tesla's first publications," Mr. Holiday caressed the volume softly. "We haven't paired him with anyone yet."

"Try Edgar Allan Poe. See if anything happens," said Dr. Violet almost jokingly. Mr. Holiday strolled the row of books until he found a collection of poems from Poe and slid the dusty Tesla book next to it on the shelf.

The spot where Mr. Holiday had placed the book suddenly brightened. An arched doorway grew into the shelf and spread wide enough for entry. "Well. Well. Look what we have here. Definitely more advanced than most places we've been. But they still have libraries with printed books. Enchanting."

Dr. Violet and I joined Mr. Holiday in the archway and peered into the brightly lit hall that reminded me of my favorite Denver Central Library. "Ohh, smell that, Dr. Violet. Intellectual life force. Mmm. It seems I'm still hungry." Mr. Holiday let his basic instinct lead him into the unknown world.

"After you, Mr. Crow," ushered Dr. Violet as he pushed me into the alien world. He knew better than to trust a panicked blood bag and wouldn't let me out of his sight. I reluctantly wandered into an unknown world between a hungry vampire and a suspicious one.

The books in this quiet library were labeled with shimmering gold titles on the spines. The letters and words had a peculiar similarity to English type with a few derivations but, for the most part, I could read them. *History of biology. Great leaders of the East Hemisphere. Planetary Wars of the Nineteenth Century.* I paused by a series of identically bound books and slid one off the shelf simply labeled with T-V. Thumbing to the last pages, I found an encyclopedic entry for Vampires.

Vampires are ancient and alien creatures. Their appearance on Trios is known to happen every 68 years. They attack randomly and drain liquids from living creatures by biting holes in the flesh. There is no known defense or cure. No known photographic evidence exists. Many witnesses claim they look like ordinary Trians.

I showed the text to Dr. Violet. He smiled and whispered, "I think we've been here before." A woman's scream broke the hush and echoed in the vast chambered hall. Mr. Holiday appeared suddenly, out of breath and nodding toward the way we came.

"They know what we are! Run!" Mr. Holiday's face emitted smoke as streaks of liquid burned into his skin at his cheeks and forehead. We all ran frantically toward the arched portal door and crashed into the dining table in the distortion bubble. Dr. Violet calmly separated the Tesla and Poe books, closed the portal, and sent the bubble on its way. Mr. Holiday snatched a black napkin from the table and vigorously scrubbed his face. "Holy water. I can't believe they knew about its use against us."

My eyes were wide as saucers as Mr. Holiday's face healed itself in seconds, the scorched flesh becoming lighter shades of pink until it finally matched his pale alabaster shade. His curled mustache and goatee grew back over the affected area until no trace of the attack remained. He smiled at me and then checked his appearance in the reflection of a silver tea saucer.

"Whew. Much more of that nonsense and I would have been in trouble," said Mr. Holiday beaming proudly at his escape.

"I don't remember that library, Mr. Holiday, but it seems we've made an impression many iterations ago," Dr. Violet pondered and then chuckled. Mr. Holiday joined him. "Renfield! Make a note in the log about Poe and Tesla. Elevate the danger level to eight."

Renfield nodded as he poured tea around the big dining table. An awkward silence fell around the room.

Only a thrumming pulse of a mysterious quantum engine barely audible tickled the eardrums to vibrate. Dr. Violet took a silent sip of tea and focused his eyes on Mr. Holiday. I guessed some sort of telepathic exchange between them. No words were spoken, yet their eyebrows wriggled as if contemplating hard choices and final decisions. Renfield went through the swinging door and allowed a gust of mechanical sounds to invade the quiet until the door closed. Then the silence returned.

I tried to interrupt the focus of the gentleman with a question. "What's been your favorite destination?" I asked hesitantly. Their eyes moved to glare at me. I deflected their stares and looked at the bookshelf with its menagerie of titles. About every fifth title had an author who was an earthling. So many alien writers, poets, and scientists filled the shelves. Likely many of those combinations led to worlds beyond my comprehension. I hoped that by keeping their memories engaged, they would be less interested in the carnal need for blood, my blood. I began to hope that I might see impossible worlds and enjoy endless exploration.

Dr. Violet followed my gaze to the books and pretended to search his memories of a place, a time, an event. Mr. Holiday's eyes remained on me. I tried to ignore his smirk and his wrinkling nose. Mr. Holiday spoke without moving his stare from my face, "I think my favorite was that industrial society in Alpha Centauri, the one with the binary suns that doubled the shadows and gave the people a skin as dark as mahogany. They relished in their technology, letting it do all their work while they basked in leisure. That's something I could get used to. I don't quite recall the book combination for that portal. One of their esteemed songstresses and an astronomer, wasn't it?" He raised his voice slightly so Dr. Violet would hear.

"Yes, I believe so. However, that system is still a long way away. We definitely should stop there and recharge ourselves when the opportunity comes," Dr. Violet replied, still scanning the endless bookshelves for other possibilities that would take less time to reach. "Renfield! Where are we in the loop and what is the next portal we have logged with available energy sources?"

Renfield popped through the swinging door and announced, "The next opportunity for a portal opening on an inhabited world is approximately two light years distant. Authors Rishmatari and Alison the Second will open the portal to the ancient tomb library of Kobtu. There is a village a few kilometers from the site. The population was approximately 3000 before your last visit."

"Two light years?" whined Mr. Holiday, "I suppose I can wait that long. Mr. Crow, here, can entertain us with his polite interrogations." His demeanor waffled between friendly and fiendish as he revealed a big smile with sharp fangs. He shifted in his velvet chair nervously like an impatient child. Then he inhaled deeply. I knew he smelled my fear and measured my response to his veiled threats to calculate the attack speed that would leave me the most vulnerable. "Maybe Mr. Crow is his generation's Einstein and can regale us with fascinating scientific theories." His stare never moved from my eyes. "Or maybe he's a poet. Are you a poet, Mr. Crow." His voice became heavy with sarcasm as if he knew I was neither, that I could not offer them great insights or recite melodic rhymes. I felt his thoughts burrow into my mind. I could sense his hunger for my life. He was eager to drain me to keep himself sustained until the next portal opened.

Dr. Violet returned to the table with an armload of books and broke the tension. "Mr. Crow. Allow me to enlighten you. While we travel in our timeless bubble, Mr. Holiday and I read extensively to keep our minds occupied." He pushed the pile of books across the table toward me. "You'd be surprised how much the mind can absorb even when the prose is unfamiliar. It's like becoming fluent in English by watching TV game shows.

This selection of books is fairly easy to decipher. They're mostly poems of heroes and their battles. Children's fairy tales." I pulled one from the top of the pile and opened it to the first page.

From Dr. Violet, I received a different vibe. His attitude suggested that I could become part of their traveling party. He wanted me to indulge in their library and become curious about life among the stars. But I saw something twinkle in his dark eyes. He was holding something back, a painful deprivation of a dark need. I knew what it was. I knew he smelled my blood. I knew neither would resist themselves when the cravings invaded their minds and overtook them. While we didn't age in the bubble, we still had to wait two years for the nearest portal opening. That's a long time to ignore the warm sustenance in the room. I sighed deeply. I didn't have long before these powerful creatures indulged their desires and drained me. Then I sighed again as my line of questioning boiled over like hate speech.

"How many worlds have you caused mass extinction events like Mica Silas?" I didn't wait for a response. "You two are monsters. You're murderers. You take indiscriminately. You eradicate intelligent life with no remorse. And then laugh about it like some tropical vacation memory. I mean, come on, back there at that last place, they fought back. You have to know you are despised for what you've become." I ended my tirade with a tantrum of toppling the stack of books onto the floor.

Dr. Violet and Mr. Holiday shared a glance before they smiled at each other and then turned their gaze to me. Mr. Holiday bared his fangs and spoke in his grumbling bear tone, "You aren't being interesting, Mr. Crow. What good are you now?"

Dr. Violet sighed and waved his hand dismissively which gave Mr. Holiday a green light to launch his attack. In a flash, he was on his feet and lunged toward me, mouth opened wide. I pushed my chair away from the table and tumbled onto the floor just before his razor-sharp teeth embedded in my throat. I scrambled under the table as Mr. Holiday jumped on top of it and waited for my head to pop up so he could slash at it with claws that had emerged from his fingertips.

I screamed, "Renfield! Protect me!" Mr. Holiday froze for a split second just as the swinging door popped open. Renfield appeared and scanned the room. I jumped from under the table and grabbed Renfield's sturdy legs while Mr. Holiday flew after me, grabbed my shoulders, and dug his claws into my winter overcoat.

"I do apologize, monsieurs," Renfield's voice was drowned out by a sudden snap of air escaping the distortion bubble. A violent rush of everything blasted into the blackness. The vampires, dining table, chairs, tea set, scones, and books all zoomed away at light speed into bits of nothing. Simultaneously, Renfield snatched me around the waist and retreated through the swinging door with my frozen, lifeless body. That was the last thing I remembered until I woke up in some sort of control room. Lights were blinking everywhere. Renfield was quickly adjusting and switching buttons and knobs. I stumbled over to where he was cycling through another round of flashing lights. "One moment, monsieur. The distortion bubble is unstable. I am attempting to reestablish the continuum. The floors shook, and the lights faded and blurred over and over. The temperature fluctuated in gradually slowing cycles from sweltering heat to frigid cold and finally eased into a numbing chill. I was glad I was still wearing my winter coat. Then, the shaking stopped, and the lights blinked less. Renfield's movements slowed to where I could watch him and not get dizzy.

"How long was I unconscious?" I mumbled to Renfield when he looked at me.

"You have been in stasis for 68 years, monsieur. We have circled the infinite loop. We will be near your home world's portal in a few months of Earth time." Renfield waited for any reaction and asked, "Would you like some tea?"

Bewildered, I nodded slowly. Then I turned toward the swinging door and pushed through. On the other side, the approximation of a French cafe appeared with an umbrella table. Bougainvillea climbed a trellis along a row of bookshelves offering its scent. The only books on the shelf were Proust's *Swann's Way* and Einstein's *Theory of Relativity*. The last combination left that would open a portal after the sudden decompression evaporated the rest of the library.

Renfield had saved my life and kept me alive until I could return to my home world. But my life stopped on Earth 68 years ago. My reality had disappeared three generations ago. The swinging door opened. Renfield brought tea and a plate of croissants. I asked him, "Is this your favorite place, Renfield?"

"Yes, monsieur. Of all the places, this felt like home." His shiny plastic face morphed into a smile.

"Come stay with me on Earth," I suggested.

"Yes, monsieur." His response was robotic, yet he seemed to know Earth would be like his home.

My messenger bag was suddenly beside me. Inside was Lovecraft's *The Shadow Over Inssmouth* and my phone. My phone still had the selfie I took with the distortion bubble library in the background. But it looked exactly like a row of books at the Denver Library . . . 68 years ago.

The Phantom of the Niebelungen

Geoffrey Hart

On those rare occasions I want culture, I buy yoghurt. Art museums? Forget about it. Stuck-up snots, and you'd need a stethoscope to find a pulse. Book readings? Not likely. About the only blood flowing's when the author cuts her finger—and it's always a *her*. Music? Ah . . . now that's another story entirely. For the right music, I'll endure culture. Take Wagner, for one. It's not that I like *opera,* you understand—I like the class of patron it attracts: emotionally uncontrolled types who know how to *feel.*

I'd been scanning that cultural desert, the newspaper's Arts section, for weeks, and today was finally the day—an announcement of the Metropolitan Opera reprise of last year's triumphal performance of the *Ring Cycle.* There'd been rumors for much longer, of course, but the director was a secrecy freak, and there'd been no way to confirm anything. I could hardly contain myself. It was like hearing your favorite restaurant was reopening after renovations. When the moment finally arrived, I was quivering with anticipation.

The Cycle begins with *Das Rheingold.* Anticipation notwithstanding, listening to the CD to prepare for the big day put me out like a light and kept me there until the alarm clock dragged me back into the day. So: *Das Rheingold.* Episode one of four is a tale about the Rhine gold, though the only gold I ever noticed in the story— back when I was paying attention to the story, that is—is the magical golden ring the Dwarf Albrecht forges in the hope he'll acquire power over the gods. Fortunately for Wagner, the best laid plans of Dwarves and men never

74

work out, as some author once noted; had they done so, it would have been a one-opera cycle, and I'd be spending more time hunting and less time dozing by the stereo.

Much though I despise the music and singing and running about and beating of breasts, it must be said the old German had an attractive take on life: The Ring cycle is a brooding and cynical commentary on how we mortals interact with and try to control the divine. Interesting notion, *control*, but those are deeper waters than I'm comfortable swimming in. What matters is that a very delightful, very rare class of person really *gets* Wagner, and I live for the moment their control breaks and they surrender to the music. You might say I make my living from repressed emotions, and if you want to call me a psychologist, guilty as charged—though between you and me, they'd drum me out of the profession so fast that *allegro* wouldn't cover it. Also, there's the inconvenient fact that I help too many people and don't charge anything for my services.

I was out taking the air that night after the performance, keenly alert after spending—*God, was it really three hours?*—marinating in the emotions permeating the opera house, appetite whetted to the point where I was past ready to dine. There'd been so many to choose from, but the one who most caught my fancy I was guessing was a banker in his late 50s. The scent of lilac lay heavy on the night air and heavy rain earlier that evening had washed away most of the smog, but what filled my tingling nostrils was the knot of emotions coiling within that tightly disciplined mind, crammed so full of statistics and Revenue Ministry regulations.

Right about now, you've probably coughed politely to yourself, muttered something about mixed metaphors, and wondered where I'm going with this. Relax. The metaphors remain happily unmixed, even if I'm taking liberties with the language. Think of it this way: Ever been in a commuter bus Monday night while the day shift heads home after a rough day, wrinkled your nostrils, and wondered why anyone wastes their time showering in the *morning*? Ever been in a locker room when the team's been playing their hearts out and still losing? Ever smelled the clenched sphincters of a bunch of religious extremists picketing the latest porno film? Yeah, *like that.* Even *you* can smell other people's emotions if you try; you just haven't really tried.

Me? I'm the Guerlain of emotions. I can smell things you didn't even know existed unless you read psych journals for the fun of it. (And if you do? Get a life.) The more complex and disturbed the mix of emotions, the more delightful. My highbrow friends stand in awe of my discerning wine palate, but they'd shun me like a skunk at a wedding if they suspected for one moment that my palate depended on how recently they'd refreshed their underarm deodorant. As "telepathy" goes, it's limited, but I get by just fine, thanks for asking.

So Banker Guy strode briskly on through the night, and I followed behind him, savoring the subtle blend of his thoughts, freighted delicately with lilac. *Nouvelle cuisine,* perhaps, but no less delicious. I began following a little more closely now, salivating. I let a deeper part of my consciousness emerge and lock onto the subtext of his thoughts, tasting the faintest residues of a deep fear the Wagner had conjured forth, the key to unlocking what I hungered after. As that part of me responded ever more strongly, I felt the first stirring of the physical changes. In the neon light from a shop window, my reflection in the armored glass had grown distinctly hunched and my face ever so slightly lupine.

So the guy had a problem with werewolves? Honestly, the people we trust with our money!

After a time, my prey turned into a tree-lined drive. By now, we'd left the theater district and come to the ritzy part of town, and a long stretch of manicured lawn fronted a distinguished old home. I paused, gauging distances, then chose my moment. Striking my best operatic pose, I pointed my muzzle at the moon and howled. The quarter moon was waning, spoiling the effect if you're a purist, but the moon wasn't the important element of our shared reality. The banker turned, eyes wide, and I sprang towards him, savoring the delirious acceleration from my powerful new muscles. With a sob of fear, he spun on his heel and ran, surprisingly fast for a man of his age and economic class. I pursued, panting harshly as I closed the distance, and he looked over his shoulder at the last possible instant. As he turned, he tripped and fell, a scream keening up into the night as I reared up over him, silhouetted artistically against what remained of the moon, fangs bared and gleaming in the pale light, claws hooked and poised to tear and rend, and . . .

All right, I confess. I have a low taste in melodrama, perhaps another reason why I find Wagner the best music to hunt by.

I felt his release wash over him. Have you ever seen a fox catch a rabbit in one of those PBS nature documentaries, and heard the rabbit scream? You have if the filmmaker's been at all honest. Now I'm no more a wildlife expert than I am a shrink, but I've always believed the rabbit screams so it won't feel the pain as the fox devours it. Call it an educated guess. The same principle applies in the martial arts: In karate, you scream when you punch. The mystics claim this ensures you'll hold nothing back of the mental energy they claim is so important to the blow. Me, I'm guessing that it just helps you ignore the pain of whacking your soft hands into some poor defenseless board or brick, but I wouldn't know—I don't fight with boards and bricks. But what I'm getting at is that the same principle applies in primal scream therapy, and I'm about as primal a therapist as you'll ever meet. So my dinner screamed, and all those delightful, painful, pathogenic stresses he'd locked up so tightly in his finely tuned mind boiled up and fled through the gateway that sound opened.

Not much escaped me. We shared his cherished image of a carefully ordered mind and life, and the smothering fear of how my rending him into itty-bitty little pieces would eradicate that order. I fed him back the image of my fangs locking onto his throat, of my claws scattering his bowels and an overpriced pre-opera dinner across the manicured lawn, and I fed gluttonously on the despair and horror. Charged with that energy, I lowered his slack but otherwise undamaged form to the ground and fled into the night, alive in the same way someone blasted on crack must be. Mind you, I've never used the stuff myself, and not from any misplaced sense of morality.

I've just found a better drug.

I ran for most of an hour, high on stolen emotions, coming back to myself only as I returned to my own neighborhood, tuxedo hanging in rags. I slept so deeply I never even heard the paper girl making her morning delivery. But the next morning, as I sipped black coffee strong enough to stand a spoon in, I saw my story. The way *they* told it, a senior accountant at some Bay Street firm (my "banker") claimed to have been followed home from the opera house and attacked by a werewolf. The writer, with tongue firmly in cheek, noted dryly how the accountant had consumed a bottle of vintage wine before attending a particularly atmospheric opera. I grinned. The accountant would recover swiftly, apart from a torn muscle sustained during the pursuit. I was pleased he'd sustained no additional injury, though it wouldn't have bothered me much or for long had his injuries been more severe. It's the nature of the predator–prey relationship, and you can't change what you are.

The police were mystified the man had been left uninjured, with no money or other valuables taken. One officer, off the record, opined that "the poor sap must've been under too much stress at work, spring being the silly season for accountants." An uncommonly perceptive guy for a cop, and so much for *that* particular stereotype. I turned to the Sports pages next, doing a little research. I manage to live modestly well by placing careful bets on local sporting events; it's a distinct advantage to know the pre-game mental states of the players and bookies when you need to beat the point spread. I could've lived much better than modestly, but I'd smelled a bookie's hunger enough times to know what would happen if I attracted their attention. I may be a monster, but that doesn't mean I'm always the apex predator in the human ecosystem.

A couple weeks later, I'd begun to feel the hunger again, but the second installment in the Ring cycle was about to begin. I made the arrangements for a new tux, purchased a ticket over the phone, and settled back to wait.

***

Episode two: *Die Walkure*. Wagner's done picking on short people, and has moved on to feminists, including the eponymous Valkyrie, Brunhilde. Said chickie disobeys her father and falls for a mortal; Odin only knows why. Politically correct this ain't. In the legend, Valkyries are tough, independent, modern bitches, the warrior women who fly fallen warriors to Valhalla, and the notion that one might give it all up for a sensitive new-age guy? Just don't go there, at least not with any women in the room. There's more gloomy Nordic stuff, but the point is, I'd be sitting with a different crowd this time, and I had a particular sort of craving. You know how some nights, nothing but a pizza and old episodes of *The Twilight Zone* will do? Or maybe it's imperial rolls and old episodes of *M*A*S*H*, bouillabaisse and *Voyage to the Bottom of the Sea*, or moussaka and the *Odyssey* in front of the fireplace. Tonight, I was hunting Valkyrie.

Sitting in the cheap seats until the singing finally ended was like waiting for a restaurant's kitchen to open—

after you've been fasting all day and just finished your annual colonoscopy, so you're as empty as empty gets. Amidst the savory stew in that enclosed space, one particular set of emotions had caught my attention. I thumbed my phone's volume higher until I'd tuned out the worst of the singing, and spent the next hour locking in on *her*, trying not to drool (it looks bad on the tux) and making sure she was alone. When the performance let out, she left by herself, lost in thought, and I had no difficulty following her.

She was Black, and from what I could tell, her particular horror was being mugged and ravished by an extravagantly unkempt white man. That appealed so much to my sense of irony that I let the transformation begin without bothering to check whether anyone else was around; it wasn't a particularly dramatic change, since all I needed to do was lengthen my hair and my legs, grow a bit of a belly, let a few days' growth of beard emerge, and snatch a wickedly sharp knife from the night air. As we walked and I slowly closed the gap between us, the quality of the neighborhood deteriorated. When she moved into a suitable gap between the street lamps, I surged after her, moving about as subtly as the morning garbage truck when the driver knows everyone's still sleeping. She heard my feet pounding the pavement, saw and mistook the nature of the lust on my face, and turned to flee, knees gone weak.

I've got to tell you, that fear response is delicious—the same thing that paralyzes a bird when it meets the eyes of a snake, and cold blood or no, the snake surely gets off on it too. I caught hold of her and pulled her into a convenient alleyway. There, I fed her mind what she wanted, vaguely repulsed by the whole thing. I suppose if you called me a voyeur, I'd be hard pressed to deny it, but let's be clear about this; I'm a *very specific* type of voyeur. It's not the sex or the violence that attracts me; it's the emotions they release. Her terror was something wholly different from the accountant's, and escaped much more slowly. I savored her, and it was more satisfying than the gluttony with which I'd devoured the accountant.

When I was done, I turned and strode away down the alley, full of the strength of the gods, Dwarvish ring or no Dwarvish ring. When the mugger came at me out of a doorway, the jagged stump of a bottle slashing for my gut, I slapped his arm aside with one hand and seized his elbow with the other. Then I closed my grip until he screamed, his agony a *lagniappe* dessert, and released him only once he'd lost consciousness and my fingers had nearly met in the middle. Don't be too quick to congratulate me; this was no vigilante justice, a concept I personally find distasteful. I simply don't like being attacked. A man's got a right to his personal space, y'know. Don't make a big deal of it.

The next day, it took a little more searching to find the news story. After all, prominent white male accountants rate considerably higher in the newspaper hierarchy than working single mothers who go without food to afford an occasional evening of opera. The same guy who'd covered the previous attack, and the several others that had preceded it over the years, hypothesized "an epidemic psychosis stalking the city," and recommended that "culture vultures with overactive imaginations" avoid Wagner for the next few weeks. His words, not mine—there are worse literary sins than mixing your metaphors. I turned to the Sports pages again, as the balloon payment on my condo was coming due and a few extra bucks wouldn't hurt.

***

Another few weeks passed, and it was time for the third of *The Ring Cycle* to take the stage. The hunting had grown lean lately, so I reserved myself a ticket, then downloaded several hours of podcasts for my phone. I ran a few errands, placed a few bets, strolled around a bit, then made my way to the opera house in plenty of time to scope out the buffet.

Something odd hung in the air that particular night, as out of place as Old Spice in the girls' locker room; it was like an aftertaste to the stew of odors circulating in the opera house's closed air, as if a chef had added curry to the spaghetti sauce instead of basil.

Act three was *Siegfried*, and this time Wagner takes a shot at the animal lovers. It just occurred to me: Maybe the reason this opera cycle is so popular is that over the course of four episodes, it manages to offend everyone? Kinda like *South Park* for the overeducated? But back to the opera. In *Siegfried*, the guy who gets star billing on the marquee hunts down and slays a giant dragon. As you might expect, the room was filled with vicarious heroes, and the mixture of testosterone and Axe aftershave was a powerful, if nauseating, stimulant. As the singers stalked about the stage, thrashing the boards, I turned up the volume and listened to John Gray explaining why Leo Buscaglia was from Venus, or something like that. By the end of the evening, I was starting to feel just a tad edgy, and resolved to stay out of the talking books section of iTunes from now on.

By then, I'd selected my victim, a thin young fellow with a disciplined mind softened only slightly by the reefer he'd smoked during the intermission. A bright guy with a rich variety of tightly closed doors that promised an abundance of controlled emotions to feed on. I guess the ambiance had gotten to me, 'cause I stalked him with brutal efficiency. Maybe it was all that testosterone; maybe it was that damned Axe he was wearing. Whatever it was, I got careless.

My dinner was one of those role-playing gamers you've probably read about, and he believed implicitly in dragons, creatures of the night, and all kinds of stuff real adults know is horseshit. I transformed faster than was comfortable, driven hard by impatient hunger, and my steps must've grown clumsy before I adjusted to my new bulk. So he heard me, and turned on his heel with surprising grace. His eyes widened as he saw me rearing above him, yard-long fangs gleaming in the streetlights and claws that would have shredded Toledo steel clashing like castanets, and as the barriers came down in his mind, I staggered back as if he'd hit me with Excalibur: *The young fool was actually preparing to attack me!*

I forgot for just the briefest moment how much of my transformation is psychological rather than physical. As I shifted gears—let's be honest, I stripped the whole damned gearbox downshifting—he stepped inside the reach of my "claws" and delivered two blows to my midsection so fast I was only able to count them by the number of times I felt ribs crack. I fell to the ground, the transformation ebbing as I lost my focus in an unfamiliar wash of pain.

Things would have been dire for me if he hadn't made the mistake of feeling elated at his victory. I can understand the reaction; by rights, what he'd seen should've run him through a Cuisinart instead of letting him drop me like a poleaxed peasant. But his elation flooded into me, and I fed that energy into the broken ribs, healing them. Then I got back on my feet and slipped into that easy empathy that would drive the change once more. His grin faded as I loomed up over him, but fortified by his previous success, he stepped back into some kind of martial arts stance and waited, mind going blank with concentration.

Great. I'd inadvertently picked Jet Li for my victim. As I mulled that over, beginning to seriously consider giving up and seeking easier prey, he took matters into his own hands. I heard his *kiai!* just as he spun into a roundhouse kick and knocked me flying against a lamp post. This time, he'd caught me in the diaphragm and it was all I could do to retain consciousness long enough to draw another breath. But his elation swelled like an orgasm, and that energy sustained me. I rose once again, unsteadily, but having learned my lesson, I found my own center first while he prepared for what should have been the *coup de grace*. As he gathered himself for the explosive release of energy in that final blow, I flowed into his mind more deeply than before, sucking in every last ounce of that release. Overconfident, he danced into some elaborate kata he'd probably learned from Hollywood, and this time, I met him midway.

Look, I'm not trying to justify what happened; it just happened. Maybe I was a little pissed at the broken ribs, maybe I was giddy from lack of oxygen and getting into the whole dragon thing too much, and maybe it was just the testosterone. I met his attack too directly, and he rebounded and hit the pavement like a sack of potatoes dropped from an airplane. That abruptly, nothing remained to feed on.

This wasn't supposed to be the way it happened. Dinner wasn't supposed to fight back, or at least not enough to get hurt. I slunk away into the night, hunger only partially satisfied. I would need to feed again far sooner than usual, and I felt like a junkie seeking some sordid kind of fix.

The furor over the kid's death took long enough to die down. I was forced to resort to some fairly objectionable means to sustain myself. I remember an old comic book about a geriatric vampire working at a blood bank to pay for his special fanged dentures and making periodic withdrawals without anyone noticing. Me, I sought out the Metro loonie bin, where the emotional energy was so intense it could recharge my batteries within minutes. Problem was, once I'd finished feeding, I was in no fit state to do much of anything but hide in my room until my personal reality conformed more closely to the social norm. The nonconformity bothered me less than the indigestion; eating at the asylum was the gastronomic equivalent of bingeing at McDonald's, without any such thing as psychic Pepto-Bismol to deal with the aftermath.

***

By the time it was once more safe to hunt my preferred prey, *The Ring Cycle* had moved into the last week of Act Four's turn on stage. *Die Gotterdammerung*, "the twilight of the gods," is Wagner's attempt to offend the religious folk. In it, all the gods and heroes die and the world ends, thank you very much and please turn out the lights when you exit the theater. The sort of plot that brought all the nihilists out of the woodworks, though I was past caring. I needed *good* food, and I needed it *now*. I selected a female victim this time, someone with a professorial sort of feel. I don't ordinarily have much in the way of preferences concerning my victim's sex, but I do fancy myself an equal-opportunity predator, and my most recent prey had been exclusively male.

By the time the show let out, I knew every song on *A Night at the Opera* by heart, but at least I was in control of myself. I stashed my phone and followed the professor slowly, savoring the moment, this time making sure everything was perfect before I pounced. University girl feared someone exactly like myself, a sort of psychic vampire, so I didn't have to change at all, other than to acquire some props. In hindsight, her thoughts should have sent me fleeing for the safety of the loonie bin cafeteria, but emotion overruled logic this time, for which I blame Freddie Mercury. (God, I miss Freddie. There was a man who wore emotion like most of us wear a parka in January.) I cleared my throat and raised my cape in billows about me as she turned. If only I'd had some dry ice, the mood would have been perfect. But things went sour immediately.

"Good evening," she said, nary a tremor in her voice. "I'd begun to doubt your existence."

"*Excuse me?*" I replied, thrown off balance. I no longer sensed any fear, and the exhilaration that took its

85

place was like drinking from what you expected to be a glass of apple juice and tasting Coke instead—the old battery acid stuff, not the new pap. It made my teeth hurt, figuratively speaking. I rallied, trying to regain control of the situation before it went completely to hell. "Lady, don't you realize that I'm going to kill you and suck out your soul?"

She laughed, clearly relieved. "*Please.* I've been following you since you started haunting the opera house last year. You've only killed one person, and I'd bet that was purely accidental. Feel free to correct me if I'm wrong . . . ?"

I frowned, now totally off my stride. "No, you're not wrong. *Damn.* You've got me at a disadvantage."

"So it would appear. But don't worry, I'm not planning to turn you in. I just want to study you."

"*Study me*? What the devil for?"

"Your existence confirms certain hypotheses about the nature of human emotion. Something I've been trying to prove in the lab, without much luck, for several years now. My postdoc funding's running low, but this—this'd mean tenure for sure!"

This woman wasn't the least bit scared of me; quite the contrary, *I* was beginning to fear her. If she turned me into some sort of lab rat, I'd be in the *Enquirer* and the *Star* right next to the UFO aliens and Bigfoot's ghost, and so much for gourmet dining ever again. The gun she pulled from her purse came almost as an anticlimax, though it took my mind off my other problems most wonderfully. I raised my arms reluctantly, then felt the intense intellectual curiosity she'd held in check until that moment beginning to seep around the edges of her control. I fed gratefully on that, unbeknownst to her, as she blathered on about what this meant for her career, how she'd put some Miller fellow in his place at last, and which journal would publish her first. When I'd fed enough, I lowered my arms.

"Keep 'em up. I won't hesitate to use this," she gestured with the gun. "I've had some Reserves training, so I'm reasonably confident I can put you down without any permanent damage. That's not to say it won't hurt like fuck."

"I believe you," I replied, advancing on her calmly, arms extended. She fired once, twice, but with the energy I'd tapped—and with more pouring out every second as her fear bubbled up—it was a simple matter to send the bullets away into the night. I gathered her into my arms, tasting her fear ever more keenly, and made with the Bela Lugosi shtick. But as I savored her growing panic, waiting for it to burst past the last of her crumbling control and fill me, a siren erupted in the next street over. I'd forgotten the gunshots! I turned at once to flee, pushing her away from me and cursing the *psychosus interruptus*, but I did not dare risk a confrontation with the police. *Perceptive* guys, yes; *sympathetic* guys, not so much.

Before I could run, she seized my arm and stepped in front of me to block my flight. I could see the excited flush in her face, and a faint sheen of sweat. "Running won't help. If you run, I'll be van Helsing to your Dracula, Ahab to your great white whale . . . I can offer you a better alternative." The gun had vanished, and with all strength gone from my limbs, she tucked my arm firmly under hers and held on as if we were nothing more than a couple out for a stroll. She began walking in the direction we'd already been headed, and I followed numbly.

The police cruiser rounded the corner in a flat skid, siren piercing my ears, but the cops spotted nothing out of the ordinary and sped on past us, accelerating. Once they were safely out of sight, I extricated my arm from her sweaty grasp and stopped walking. "You mentioned an alternative?"

She smiled, and I could smell her relief. "Yes. Join me at the university. My funding's a shambles, but I never managed to spend my budget for a research assistant.

And they won't let me spend it on anything practical, like food. You're uniquely qualified to help me in my work."

"Which is?"

"The psychology of emotion. I run student volunteers through a bunch of tests and measure their electromagnetic responses, but I've always felt I've been missing something—it's like they're too damned controlled, and not a one of them knows how to let go and really *feel*. So I don't get the signal strength I need. I've a notion you could help me with that."

I neglected to point out that trying to explain emotions in terms of electromagnetics was like blaming urban crime on Democrats. "Yes, I probably could. But what's in it for *me*?"

"Apart from the stipend? Well, for one thing, a steady and diverse diet. You'll never want for nourishment if you hang around the campus. And the lab work is just an appetizer . . . you ought to see what students go through around exam time." Her smile broadened, and there was something cold in it that I liked. "Plus, if you think these opera buffs are juicy bundles of stress, you're going to love thesis defenses and board of governors meetings." She laughed. "This could be the start of a beautiful friendship, Louis."

"Frank." I laughed back at her, my apprehension easing slightly, and put my arm protectively around her waist. "Nothing pretentious about Bogie. You have to respect that."

She slipped her arm around my waist and squeezed. "We're going to have some interesting times ahead, Frank."

The fat lady had sung, and the opera was over. But something else was starting here, and I had the feeling I was going to like it a whole lot better than Wagner.

Author and Artist Bios

Francis Wesley Alexander is a seven-time *Rhysling* nominee and three-time *Dwarf Stars* nominee. He is the author of *When the Mushrooms Come,* and *I Reckon,* and coeditor with Theresa Santitoro of the *Drabbun Anthology.* Wes has been published in *Hungur Chronicles*, *Martian Wave, The Fifth Di, Tales from the Moonlit Path, Valley Voices, Cattails, The Pan Haiku Review, Scifaikuest*, and *Horror Senryu Journal.*

Andrage Benedik, a promising literary voice originating from Slovenia, has passionately cultivated narratives that traverse the juncture of fantasy and science fiction. With a commendable track record of published works in their native language, Andrage is working to bring their English works to a wider audience, aiming to inspire and connect with readers on a global scale. Their tales try to shed a light on society, the people that reside within it, and the bonds they forge, through the lens of speculative fiction.

Marcia A. Borell is happily enjoying her 70th decade. She continues to make marvelous artistic messes and to drag the stories out of her head and into words strung together on paper or the computer. Drabbles and haibuns are her favorite forms.

She also finds ways to nurture her world. Summers are spent in the garden and the greenhouse caring for monarch caterpillars and butterflies.

James W. Bullard lives in Colorado with his girlfriend, his son, and a spoiled Aussie shepherd. Writing is a hobby along with watercolor painting and drinking craft beer. His sci-fi novel, *The Engine Key,* is available on Amazon.

Gary Davis loves all things classic horror, including vampires, werewolves, mummies, ghosts, and Halloween. Regarding vampires, he prefers to write about the highly predatory, rat-like Nosferatu-style creature rather than the Lord Byron-style romantic type. The Nosferatu vampire has a stronger connection to the East European folkloric vampire of several centuries ago, when "vampires" were sometimes plague victims who were alleged to return from the grave to infect other people. Plague, of course, was often carried by rats.

The Nosferatu vampire, materializing from ether in a graveyard, is featured in Mr. Davis' poem, "Gothic Night," published in *Tales of the Talisman* (2014). He has other poetry (including haiku) published in *The Hungur Chronicles*, *Tales from the Moonlit Path*, *Tales of the Talisman*, *Bloodbond*, *Illumen*, *Scifaikuest*, *Star*Line*, *Zen of the Dead*, *Lupine Lunes*, *It Came from her Purse*, *Spaceports & Spidersilk*, *Potter's Field 7* and a sci-fi anthology, *Kepler's Cowboys* (2015-2023). Mr. Davis has published Halloween short stories in *Frostfire Worlds*, *Spaceports & Spidersilk,* and *Potter's Field 7* (2016-2021). He published a short story about vampires on the Moon and an article, "Severed Heads and Omens of Death: The Horror Origins of Halloween," in the Samhain 2022 issue of *The Hungur Chronicles*.

Geoff Hart has reputedly been telling tales (sometimes ending up in considerable trouble thereby) since he was 6, but took nearly 20 years to realize that he could earn a living at this trade. Since 1987, he's worked as a technical writer and scientific editor for IBM, the Canadian Forest Service, and the Forest Engineering Research Institute of Canada. Since 2004, he's been a freelancer, and only occasionally stops complaining about his boss. Geoff has worked primarily as a scientific and technical editor, specializing in authors who have English as a second language, but also does technical writing and French translation. He claims to have survived at least two bouts of leading or managing publications groups with only a minor need for ongoing therapy. A Fellow of the Society for Technical Communication (STC, www.stc.org), he has published more than 450 nonfiction articles on communication as well as the books *Effective Onscreen Editing*, *Writing for Science Journals*, and *Write Faster With Your Word Processor*. He spends an altogether unreasonable amount of time mentoring colleagues. His training is in plant ecology and plant physiology, which fascinate him. In his spare time, he has committed three SF novels and a short story collection, and has sold 63 stories. Visit him online at <www.geoff-hart.com>.

David Lee Summers lives in Southern New Mexico at the cusp of the western and final frontiers. He's written novels about space pirates, vampire mercenaries, mad scientists in the old west, and astronomer ghosts. He's edited thrilling anthologies of space adventure that imagine what worlds discovered by NASA's Kepler mission might be like. Watch for his new novel, *Ordeal of the Scarlet Order*, coming soon from Hadrosaur Productions. When he's not writing or editing, David explores the universe for real at Kitt Peak National Observatory. To learn more about David or his books visit his website at http://www.davidleesummers.com

The Dead Seas - Nick Sea & Suzie Sea: The married artists are based in Louisville and create original collaborative paintings in a unique combination of traditional fine art and surreal art styles.

The website for their work: www.thedeadseas.art